the Long Goodnight

the Long Goodnight

WE'RE NOT TROUBLEMAKERS
WE'RE TROUBLE **FINDERS**.

TYLER
TORK

an imprint of
Roan & Weatherford Publishing Associates, LLC
Bentonville, Arkansas
www.roanweatherford.com

Library of Congress Cataloging-in-Publication Data
Names: Tork, Tyler, author.
Title: The Long Goodnight/Tyler Tork | The Goodnight Agency #2
Description: First Edition. | Bentonville: Mad Cat, 2024.
Identifiers: LCCN: 2024947575 | ISBN: 979-8-89299-006-6 (trade paperback) |
ISBN: 979-8-89299-007-3 (eBook)
Subjects: | BISAC: YOUNG ADULT FICTION/Fantasy |
YOUNG ADULT FICTION/Paranormal, Occult & Supernatural |
YOUNG ADULT FICTION/Fantasy/Dark Fantasy
LC record available at: https://lccn.loc.gov/2024947575

Mad Cat trade paperback edition October, 2024

Cover & Interior Design by Casey W. Cowan
Illustrations by: cxojinu
Editing by Mari Mason, Laura Lauda & Amy Cowan

To all those who don't fit in,
and fight for justice.

One

By the end of her martial arts lesson, Ruby Park was sweaty, bruised, and a little tired of being snapped at—this foot here, crouch lower, arm held so. Her instructor, Master Ujo, was a tiny ball of blue fury while the lesson was in progress. Outside of lessons, though, he was the most tentative creature Ruby knew. She almost charged right out to the showers without realizing he had more to say, but something about his posture, his standing almost in the path to the door, and the way he carefully wasn't looking at her, made her wonder.

"Was there something else?"

The cilia around the little niovi's mouth quivered, and the one big eye in the middle of his narrow blue face looked up into hers briefly. "You spoke on the phone earlier."

Had she? When? Oh, when she'd entered, she'd been on a call. "Yeah, but I know the rule. I turned it off right away once I got inside. I just had to arrange with a friend for a ride after the lesson."

"You called him Kirk."

"Yes, it was Kirk." What was this about?

"The one who helped slay the beast?"

Several weeks ago, Ruby had gotten together a team of kids to take out a mostly invisible monster that had been eating people, that the adults weren't dealing with. "Yes, he was a huge help."

"I heard he fought the creature with a sword?"

"The moon sword, yeah, but he didn't hurt it much. It was the explosives that finished the job."

Ujo stared at his feet.

"Did you, uh, want to meet him when he shows up?" The Scene, a hidden society of oddball creatures and recluses, was so full of secrets that many of its members didn't even know some of the others existed. You always had to ask before introducing someone— especially a human.

"I could. I could meet him."

Did that mean he really wanted to? Or was he just feeling pressured now since she'd suggested it? "I should ask him in?"

"If he wishes."

Kirk would definitely be interested, and so far he'd been able to resist any temptation he might have felt to spill all the cool secrets he'd learned. And Ujo had brought it up. "I'll send him up when he arrives."

She'd normally hit the showers before going downstairs and out to the street, but if Kirk was already there, she didn't want to make Ujo wait. Also, she needed to see what this was about.

Kirk was out front, waiting on a bus stop bench in the broiling sun, reading a comic book. His curly orange hair stuck out from beneath a Windy City Rollers baseball cap—reversed, of course. He looked around when she hissed at him.

"Come up, my teacher wants to see you."

"Me?" Kirk stood, putting the comic in his satchel, and came into the tiny vestibule. Ruby had held the door open so she wouldn't have to re-enter the code, and she let him pass so she could pull it shut and make sure it latched. Crowded together, she was uncomfortably conscious of being disheveled and sweaty from the lesson. She led the way up the stairs to a hallway with doors leading into the studio and dressing rooms. "Let me do the talking at first, okay? He's pretty shy."

"Okay, but what does he want with me?"

Ruby shrugged, opened the door into the studio, and ushered him in.

"BOY!"

Kirk and Ruby both jumped. Master Ujo stalked across the floor mats, a curved rattan practice sword in each hand. "I hear you're pretty good with a sword." He extended one to Kirk.

"Uh...."

"Come, come. I want to see what you can do."

He glanced at Ruby, who shrugged. He took the wooden handle. "I thought we were just talking, but okay. I don't have a, a uniform or whatever you call it."

Ujo's cilia bristled. "If you are attacked, do you think your attacker will give you time to change clothes? Come at me." He stepped back several paces.

"Don't let his size fool you." Ruby gave Kirk a little push toward his much shorter opponent. "You're not going to hurt him, so don't hold back."

"I see what you mean about his shyness." Kirk stepped forward and whipped his wooden sword around a couple of times, then made a halfhearted swipe at Ujo's midsection.

It was nice to watch Ujo's Yoda-like moves from a distance for a change, instead of being their target. There was a thwack, an "Ow," and another three hits in quick succession. Kirk retreated, shielding with his sword and rubbing his thigh. He looked warily at his opponent, now.

Ujo stood there just as if he'd never moved. "You can do better. Guard yourself!" And he ran at Kirk, sword held out sideways.

The exchange this time included more wood on wood than on flesh, lasting a few seconds until Kirk got a bonk on the head which sent him staggering back. Ujo darted in and swept his feet—he landed with a grunt, then lay still looking at the niovi standing above him, point held against his chest.

Ujo stepped back, extending a hand. "Not too awful. You'll do."

Kirk hesitated, took the offered hand, and got to his feet. "I'll do for what?"

"Ruby's opponents will not all be small like me. She needs a tall sparring partner, to not learn bad habits. As I have no other students at the moment to match her against, you may also attend lessons." Ujo looked at the floor, suddenly bashful. "No charge. If that will be acceptable."

Ruby was both pleased and appalled. Pleased, because Kirk would probably enjoy the lessons, and she would like having him there. Appalled, because he would think she'd asked Ujo to make the offer and because it would mean a lot of touching. That would surely seem to Kirk like encouragement, when she'd been trying to keep distance and have things stay on a "just friends" footing.

Kirk glanced at her. Seeking permission? She kept her face neutral. He faced Master Ujo. "I'll have to think about it."

The instructor was back. "Think fast. I'll want you to begin immediately to practice together for next week. You may go."

"Um, right. Does one bow or… something?"

"One just goes." He looked at Ruby. "Show him the first two forms."

Kirk looked over his shoulder as she led him back to the lobby. "Well, that was a shorter and more painful visit than I expected."

"He'll talk more once he gets to know you better."

"Would it be okay? I mean, I'd like to take him up on it if you agree."

Ruby sighed. "I have to shower and change. We'll talk on the way."

She *did* need a sparring partner if Ujo said so. Probably more than one because she wasn't sure how she was going to prepare for opponents of different shapes and numbers of limbs. Also, Uncle Simon was paying more than a little—to judge by his expression when he'd opened the invoice—for her to get this training. If it was that valuable, it would be unreasonable to ask Kirk to pass up a chance to get it for free.

She came out into the lobby, stuffing her damp hair into a scrunchy. Kirk pulled down his shirt sleeve where he'd been examining one of his new bruises and held the door for her as they left. "What do you think?"

"Fine. It'll be fun." Ruby touched the handle of her own practice sword, strapped under her backpack. "Do you have one of these?"

"Yes, but mine is straight. We use them in SCA. But I thought you were learning hand to hand."

She went ahead of him down the stairs. "The stuff he asked me to show you first is hands and feet, but it's a little of everything." She touched the little tube on her backpack strap. "We're even training Speck on some new moves."

Hearing his name, Ruby's ghost dog popped out, hovering in front of her face. She waved him back into the tube. He was mostly invisible, but the little shimmer still occasionally drew attention from mundanes, so she kept him hidden in public.

As they emerged onto the sidewalk, Kirk pointed. "Car's that way. It seems like you have different lessons all day long. You must be about ready for school to start so you don't have to study so hard."

"You're a smartass, but you're not wrong. My brain is pretty much always full. But it's fun. And music is still part of it, at least."

"Speaking of which, I have a new song. Sent you email. And M has an idea for one, so we're meeting at Revenge at eight. Can you make it?"

"If you don't mind me studying accounting while you guys work on it." Recognizing Kirk's beat-up Honda Civic, she stopped by the passenger door. While waiting for him to unlock it, she turned on her phone—Ujo insisted it be turned off during lessons, not just silent. It immediately dinged. "Wow."

"Wow, what?"

"I got a calendar invite from Uncle Simon, seven p.m., subject, 'Friggin Skohlars.'"

"The rat people? What's up with them?"

The lock clicked, and she pulled the door open. "Don't call them rats. They don't like it. I don't know, this is the first I've heard about them in a while. But Simon never schedules things at mealtimes and never swears. It must be pretty important."

"'Friggin' is a pretty mild oath."

"Even so, he didn't just say it. He typed it." She tapped Accept. "So I might be a little late tonight."

Kirk shrugged as he pulled out into traffic. "When the boss calls…."

It was only about three o'clock, but outdoors it was nearly dark, the sky overcast and green. Standing in the conservatory of Ms. Wheelwright's house, Marissa Gomez watched the coming storm. Around and under the perfectly manicured topiary and shrubs, in the shadows, vague lights floated. They drifted randomly, apparently immune to the rising wind that tossed and shivered the plants. Pixies—or so she'd been told, though it was possible Ithikate was testing her credulity.

She walked back to the little table at the center of the large, glass-walled room. She had her choice of places to practice and had chosen this place for its warmth and the little bit of outside noise that filtered in—birds, airplanes, and, now, wind. The rest of the house was either too quiet or too full of noise—human and otherwise—for her to focus.

She sat at the table, closed her eyes, and controlled her breathing. In, out, slowly. Ms. Wheelwright seemed confident that Marissa could learn to do as she did, to see the world from "underneath," by symbols and hints, to trace the struts and levers of cause and effect and try shifting them to "tweak" future events to a desired outcome. There should be some little thing she could do, some domino she could knock over, to start the chain of events, even without knowing exactly how her actions would bring that about. Someone she should talk to, some little apparently unrelated action.

At least, Ms. Wheelwright thought she should be able to. Marissa wasn't so certain. Sure, she could visualize herself dropping, seeing the world from below, picture the connections, shift things to see what happened. But was she seeing something real or just imagining what she'd been told to expect? The only way to be sure was to try to cause something. So she had an assignment—get the letter carrier to deliver them someone else's mail tomorrow.

When she opened her eyes, William stood before her. The old butler had an uncanny knack for appearing suddenly—probably not supernatural, but with this crowd you could never be sure. "There's a guest to see you in the withdrawing-room."

"All right." Marissa stood, bracing herself on the table against the dizziness that always followed her attempts at this stuff, and followed the antique servant into the echoing main hall, around the stacks and cabinets and sculptures that littered the floor, to a room with gold-painted trim, heavy curtains, and spindly furniture upholstered in dark red velvet. A tall, pale, dark-haired girl stood as they entered.

"Olga, hi." Marissa turned to William. "Thanks, I'll take it from here. But could you have Ithikate bring in some drinks? Lemonade for me, and...?" She looked at Olga.

"Lemonade is fine."

William nodded and left. Marissa crossed the room to give a brief hug of greeting. "Hey. Thanks for coming."

"You said there was a job, of course I came. This is some place!"

"Yeah. Wait until you see the catwalks." Marissa sat and signaled Olga to do the same. Outside, the rain began with a rattle on the windowpane.

"Is that a real Brâncuşi out there? You don't live here, do you? I thought your dad ran a garage or something."

"I don't live here, but the job is here. I just wanted to prepare you before you talk to Ms. Wheelwright. She's a little… unexpected. The other residents take getting used to, too."

"Okay. What's the job?"

"It's sort of a maid and errand person."

Olga's eyes narrowed. "Maid? They want me to clean?"

"Probably not much. They need you for other things. See, there are only a few humans living here, and they need someone who can answer the phone and the door—it's not really William's job—go out for groceries, run to the bank, serve food if there are guests, sometimes. The previous person landed an internship at some law firm. The non-humans can clean."

"What are you talking about, non-humans? Wait a minute, is this a Skohlar house? I hate those little f—"

"Not Skohlars. Didn't Ruby tell you there were several different species living in secret around here?"

"She did, but I only met one other, and it ate my friend. So I wasn't really looking to meet more."

"That was an animal. These are people. The reason you're up for this job is that you're already in on the secret somewhat. But they're going to test you. One of the staff will be here in a minute, and I need you to not freak out. All right?"

Olga gripped the arms of her chair, rising an inch. "What do you mean? What sort of thing is coming in here?"

"Her appearance is a little alarming, but Ithikate is nice. She writes poetry. She, uh, loves the TV show *Alf*, has the whole run on DVD. She's a Bears fan. She makes delicious little lavender candies. Now please settle down because I hear her coming."

A soft patter from the hallway paused, and the girls turned to watch the door edge open. A single, slender, golden-furred leg came through the opening, three toes splaying out on the hardwood floor. Then the door bumped open, and Ithikate waltzed in. Olga made a peep of dismay, but nothing worse. Marissa gave her an unobtrusive thumbs-up.

She'd considered which of the inmates to introduce first. Ithikate wasn't the scariest looking but was challenging enough to be a fair test. Five feet high with the tray held overhead, her limbs—three above, three below—were each dyed a different pastel color. The cylindrical body, with fur its natural off-white, was encircled by a row of round black eyes. Her "hips," top and bottom, were modestly covered with ruffled black pantaloons. She moved toward them with a rotary gait, smoothly, and set the tray on a little table.

"Kate, this is Olga. She's interviewing for the maid's job."

Ithikate tilted to give Olga the once-over.

Marissa reached for the frosty pitcher. "Will you sit with us a little while?"

Ithikate bobbed, then rolled to the nearest empty chair, ending upside-down from her previous orientation, three limbs folded neatly underneath and three draped over the chair arms. The row of black eyes blinked at them.

Olga took a glass from Marissa. "S-so. I hear you like the Bears."

After her Spanish lesson, Ruby had to hurry home for the meeting. She planned to leave again right after, so she stopped to pick up tacos and got in the door right at 7:02. Simon was sitting on the desk in his study, and there were two other people—Captain Susan Urbana, head of the Guardians, the Scene's police force, and Dr. Reginald Sin, an elderly Indonesian man with a tidy white beard, whom she'd last seen in this same room conducting her trial for disobedience, disrespect, and talking too much—the usual offenses where she was concerned. However—she searched her conscience and her memory—she hadn't done anything recently to merit their attention.

She stood in the doorway, looking at this little group who looked back at her. Was Captain Urbana always that cross, or was it only when

Ruby was around? At least Dr. Sin gave her a grave little smile. Simon pointed to her taco bag. "If you're thinking of setting that greasy thing down anywhere in here…"

"Just a sec." She left the bag on the kitchen counter and hurried back. "Sorry I'm late."

Simon waved her to a chair. "Sorry for the short notice. We have a job for you, unfortunately."

Captain Urbana crossed her arms. "This is a mistake."

Dr. Sin had been standing by the bookshelves, examining the rows of old leather-bound tomes. He came over and sat. "We've been through this, Susan. Much as we might like to have someone more experienced—"

"It's not just a matter of experience. It's about responsibility."

Simon waved Susan down. "It's already decided, and we're not rehashing it for the fifth time with her here. Ruby, we've hit a hitch in our negotiations with the Skohlars. What it comes down to is this— they're only willing to talk if you're there."

"What! But why?"

"Why, indeed." Captain Urbana ran a hand through her hair, leaving it disarranged. "They trust you. They say you're the only one who's taken your agreements with them seriously and succeeded in carrying them out."

"I can't be the only one. They make deals all the time, don't they? They hired someone to build their monster cages and stadium. And to fill them with monsters."

"That may be," Urbana said. "But we wouldn't have those people negotiate for our side. In fact, if we catch them, they'll be very sorry. Transporting dangerous beasts across planes… just for starters."

"I believe," said Dr. Sin, "the Skohlars also respect that you took great risks on their behalf. Whatever their reasons, they are insistent. I can fill you in on where we stand, and you can join our team at the next meeting."

"Our team—who's that?"

"The three of us."

Ruby looked at them each in turn. "Okay…." She kicked her feet. "I have a few questions, though. First, why is it only humans on this team?"

There was silence, which grew from long to uncomfortably long. Ruby waited.

"Well." Simon shifted his seat on the desk. "It is our planet."

Ruby cocked her head. "We're the only intelligent native species? I thought the Sasquatches, the Kraken—"

"Yes, yes." Urbana waved a hand. "The Skohlars themselves appear to be native, for that matter. It's a matter of who's in charge of the place, not who grew up here."

"It's about power, then. They have to deal with us because we have numbers and weapons on our side. Sort of like Europeans and Native Americans. I can't imagine why they don't trust us."

"It's not at all the same—"

"Susan." Dr. Sin raised his voice. "It's a legitimate point. From the Skohlars' point of view—"

Captain Urbana crossed her arms. "You two are always trying to shut me up. We have their best interests in mind."

"Yes," Simon said. "We do. And we need a strategy to get them to believe that. Ruby has a point. Let's propose to the Skohlars to also add a nonhuman to the negotiations."

"It couldn't hurt." Dr. Sin steepled his fingers, tapping them against his chin. "Whom could we suggest? Probably not a Sasquatch, since one of them tried to frame them for the monster attacks. Seymour's no longer in town, I suppose?"

"Gone home." Simon pulled his little black book from his jacket pocket and leafed through it. "No reason it has to be a native species, just someone smart and fair who already knows about the Skohlars. Hm. Ekikitawami Abroft?"

"The Wibble leader?" Sin nodded. "We could work with that, I guess. Susan?"

"So now you're asking my opinion? If we have to invite someone, I suppose we could do worse than Abroft."

"Great." Simon picked up a clipboard and made a note. "I'll call tomorrow and make sure they're willing. Ruby, what's your next question?"

He was looking at her. She'd raised a point, and they'd actually taken it seriously and done something about it. Holy crap!

What was her next question? "Um, yeah. Okay. Exactly what is it we want them to agree to?"

Dr. Sin raised his phone. "You'll need to study our notes. I'll email them to you."

"Sure, okay, great. I don't have any other homework."

"Treat this as a priority," Simon said. "The key points are, we want them to end the monster fights and stop stealing."

"Huh. Okay. I think the fights will end anyway now you've cut off their monster supply, but isn't stealing stuff kind of what they do?"

Urbana snorted. "We don't expect them to completely stop. We'll be happy if they keep it down to a dull roar. But don't tell them that. You don't open a negotiation with what you'll settle for. We need room to let them bargain us down."

Ruby's phone dinged, and Dr. Sin looked up from his. "There you go. Treat this as highly confidential, understood?"

"Got it."

Ruby arrived at the coffeehouse late. Kirk and Marissa were already sitting on the ratty old couch, heads together over the coffee table. Ruby stopped to stare at Marissa—at her new look. Buzz-cut hair with a purple streak, silver-edged vest over a tight black top, black jeans, black pearl stud earrings, and there was something different about her makeup too, adding more cheekbone to her cheerful round face. At least the cheerfulness was still there—Marissa looked up at her and grinned.

"Nice haircut." Ruby set her bag on the table and sat in the armchair across from them. "What do your parents think of it?"

"We're not talking about that. We're making up a song list. With the two new ones we're working on now, we should have enough to make an album."

"O... kay, and why do we want to do that?"

Kirk pushed the song list over to her. "Because it's super cool to have an album. Also, we make way more money on an album sale than from YouTube views."

"What does Wally say?" The band's fourth member, who collaborated with them from his secluded home in the Ozarks, never appeared in public.

Marissa stood, looking at the coffee menu above the counter. "We only just started talking about it. I'll email him later. Can I get you something?"

"Yes, please, a plain iced. And what would the band name be on this album?"

Kirk shrugged. "I think it would have to be the same as the YouTube channel, so we could link it from there."

"This would be the channel you created with the name you liked."

"And which Marissa now also likes."

Does she, indeed. Ruby turned to look at her, standing at the counter waiting to order. With her new semi-goth look. "I guess I'm outvoted."

"They're both good names. It would just be silly to change now when we're already getting some play as Gizmo Government. See, I made sample cover art."

"I'm not good enough to be on an album." Ruby unzipped her bag. "I'm embarrassed now at the stuff we put online. And we can't do live performances since Wally can't come out."

"People love the stuff we put online because it's funny, and the playing isn't that bad. We'll discuss it more later. We have to re-record everything with the new sound equipment anyway."

Marissa returned with three cups. Ruby grabbed the one that was most precariously balanced. Marissa set the others down, looking at the computer Ruby had taken from her backpack. "Hey, when did you get that?"

Ruby moved the notebook farther from the coffee. "I bought it with money from the Skohlar job."

Kirk grabbed his cup. "That reminds me—what did Simon want with you?"

"I, uh, can't say."

"More secrets?" Marissa tore open one sugar and one pink sweetener. "You're getting more like Simon every day."

"Sorry, I'd tell you if I could. What about you, though? How'd it go with Olga?"

"She got the job, she'll live in the house, and go to our school."

Ruby reached for a napkin. "Seriously? I thought she was dropping out."

"Ms. W won't let her. As long as she's working there, she has to be a student. Ms. W will pay her tuition, same deal as me. Then probably art school here in town, since that's Olga's thing."

"That's good of her," Kirk said. "But I thought your school was hard to get into."

Marissa smelled her coffee and smiled. "It is, but Ms. W has pull, and they have a diversity outreach thing."

Ruby cocked her head. "But she's white."

"Income diversity. I think she'll need help to catch up to the rest of the class. Her old school sounds horrible. Ms. W asked me to tutor her."

"Huh. And did you solve your prognostication puzzle?"

"It's not really prognostication. I can never tell whether I'm just imagining things, but I did come up with something."

"Which was…?"

"I felt like I should throw a croquet ball into the neighbor's yard."

"And did you?" Kirk asked.

"I felt kind of silly, but yeah, I did. I guess tomorrow when the mail comes, we'll see whether it worked. I don't see why it should, but Ms. W says it's often like that. Oh, and before I forget"—Marissa grabbed her purse and held out a card-shaped envelope to Ruby—"this is for you."

"It's not my birthday." Ruby opened the envelope and pulled out a stiff rectangle, a form engraved on one side in script font, with spaces filled in by hand. "Huh. I'm summoned to the presence."

Kirk took the card. "Dinner tomorrow at Ms. W's? How do you rate? I didn't think she liked you."

"No, our styles are incompatible. I guess this is business. Last time she invited me, she'd had a vision about me. Or not a vision, but whatever she does."

Marissa hung her purse on the chair arm. "Will you go?"

"I suppose. I hear the food is good, and I'm curious who else will be there."

"Great! Then I'll see you there." Marissa picked up the paper with the song list. "Now, let's figure out what order we should put these on the album."

Two

In her dream, Ruby stood at the peak of a roof. Micah sat farther down the roof-line, beside the chimney. He'd taken off his shirt to use for seat padding. The neighborhood below looked familiar—it was her own. They were on Uncle Simon's row house, at the end of a row of five.

Micah turned to face her, grinning from behind a mop of frizzy copper hair. His skin was bronze, and a thick mat of darker red hair covered his chest. She was almost getting used to his caveman-like face. He wasn't exactly human, but nobody had ever explained to her what he exactly was—or had been, when still alive.

He patted the roof beside him, and Ruby walked over, arms out for balance. The wind carried his scent to her—sweaty, a little sharp, a hint of patchouli. She handed him her guitar—which had been his when he was alive—and sank to a sitting position. "When I dream about you, you're always on a roof."

"Is that so?" He ran a thumb over the strings, one by one, testing the tuning, and tightened one. "I guess it's because of my religion."

"What religion is that?"

"I'm a Frisbeetarian. We believe that when you die, your soul flies up"—he lifted a hand—"and gets stuck on the roof."

"Very amusing. But why's it a different roof than before?"

He strummed a couple of chords before passing the guitar back to her. "It's your dream. What do you think?"

Before, she'd seen him atop flat-roofed buildings, like the view from her old apartment in New York, but she hadn't lived there for years. Now…. "Maybe I see you on my home. Whatever that is at the moment."

Micah bobbed his head. "Maybe. So you're feeling like this is home now?" He tapped the end of the guitar, a beautiful, red-lacquered electric with flames in gold flake. "What songs have you learned?"

What was the most impressive song she could play passably well? She took a breath and launched into "Night of the Platypus"—words by Marissa, music by Kirk. It used her new minor chords, which she adored. Dream guitars were no less recalcitrant than real-life guitars—though they sounded great even without an amp—so there were a couple of missteps, but she got through it. "I can do better. I haven't had much time to practice with all the other training."

Micah shook his head. "Never apologize, never make excuses. Nice lyrics. And you were great."

"I was?"

"No, only adequate, but it's not your job to say so. You are improving, though. And if someone *tells* you you were great, 'I was?' is the wrong answer."

Ruby thought for a moment. "How about, 'Thank you?'"

"Much better. Act like you're great, or no one else will think so."

"Okay." Ruby played the opening bars of "Auntie Gravity," a slower number inspired by her Aunt Edith. "Thanks. Did you know Simon keeps your skull on the mantel?"

"Does he? More macabre than I'd have expected of him, but I'm not using it anymore, so I suppose it's okay. It's nice to be remembered.

By the way, thanks for speaking English. Last time I totally couldn't understand you."

"When did I not speak English?"

"Last time I saw you. You're part Korean, right? I assumed it was that."

"My father was from Korea, but he died when I was three, and I don't remember much of the language."

"So it wasn't you, then? Funny, she looked like you. But things are strange here."

She put her hand across the strings, stilling them, and stared at him. "Where do you come up with these things? This is *my* dream. Am I really talking to you or just dreaming what I think you would say?"

"How would you know whether to believe my answer?"

A good point. "Tell me something I don't know, then. How did you die?"

Micah looked off, at the roof across the street. "Better you don't concern yourself with that. Anyway, it's time to wake up."

"I think that's for me to de—" But she was alone, in bed, looking at the glowing red numbers on her clock. 6:29 a.m. She flipped the alarm off before it could sound and sat up, searching the floor for her slippers by feel. She reached for her phone and texted Marissa—she wouldn't be up yet, but she'd get it eventually.

Do u believe in ghosts?

The answer came while she was brushing her teeth at the little sink in her bedroom.

No, U?

Ruby texted back, one-handed.

No but guitar maybe haunted. U up early....

After they confirmed their plans for later, Ruby checked her calendar. Spanish lesson—it was a popular language in The Scene. Secret History with Alice. Lunch with Captain Urbana, to get caught up on the Skohlar negotiations. *That* ranked somewhere below dental appointment on the scale of fun ways to spend time. Urbana clearly considered her a loose cannon, and she thought Urbana had a stick up her butt, and neither of these things was a secret to the other person.

Anyway. Band practice at two. Study time. Cultural Flexibility Dinner canceled in favor of Ms. W's. She hadn't gotten a chance to tell Simon about that because he was still out when she went to bed. She hoped he'd agree—it was bound to be tastier than whatever he had planned. Last week, it'd been Sasquatch-style beetle paste with honey-coated mushrooms on the side.

She walked softly downstairs and into the study. The house was quiet—that would change after eight a.m. The last several weeks it'd been like Grand Central every day, with a backlog of business from Simon's regulars who'd had to wait while he was in jail, plus new clients who'd previously been working with the recently deceased Alasdair Polacek.

Most of the visitors weren't clients, of course—few of those could come out during the day, which was why they needed Simon's help in the first place. Simon was their connection to humans they needed things from—accountants, realtors, contractors, perplexed grocers. He preferred to schedule meetings with them in his home office rather than running all around town.

Of course, that meant the house was on nearly constant lockdown, the weird stuff hidden away to avoid puzzling the mundanes. Including Micah's nonhuman-shaped skull on the mantel. She reached up to touch its sloping forehead. "Mystery man," she whispered. "What happened to you?"

If she stopped talking to him, maybe he'd quit visiting her dreams. Would that be a good thing? She sighed, went out to the hallway, and pressed the hidden stud in the staircase carving. The floor vibrated slightly as lockdown began. If she returned to the study now, Micah would be gone. But she didn't—instead she headed through the old-fashioned dining room to the thoroughly modern kitchen. If she hustled, she'd have a free hour before needing to run for the train.

She should probably use that time to practice guitar. If they really were doing that album, she needed to get better in a hurry. On the other hand, sitting in the gazebo reading sounded awfully nice before a busy day.

Marissa was, let's face it, not the world's greatest soccer player. She wasn't especially fast or strong and sometimes got confused and lost track of the ball. But playing was fun, and being on a team was terrific. Since her dad was coach and sponsor, it also gave her a chance to spend time with him, when he was otherwise always at work.

Not that they were on speaking terms at the moment, due to the "savage butchery" of her new haircut. Still, she'd made the team again this year, and he'd get used to her new look. Kirk had certainly noticed and commented on it last night. Working together on the album would be great.

After practice, she caught a train. Ms. W's mansion was in the northern part of the city, the only house in its neighborhood with a huge yard and high stone privacy fence. The neighbors on either side had spike-fenced yards, but nothing to compare, and the rest of the area was mixed, with small older houses, a couple of low-rise apartment buildings, row houses, shops, a school. Not a bad area, though a little tame and extremely white.

Marissa let herself in with the keypad code, then checked the mailbox, which could only be emptied from inside the wall. The mail had already come—advertising, a catalog, statements, a dozen letters from charities, no doubt seeking donations. Unfortunately, all were addressed to Ms. W or her nephew—nothing misdelivered.

She sighed. She got the sense that Ms. W was starting to doubt her choice of a protégé, and this wasn't going to help. Though it might actually be a relief if it didn't work out. It was important to do things you weren't good at because how else would you get good? But she didn't seem to be improving at this tweaking thing, and it might be time to cut her losses. Ms. W would just have to resume her long-running search for someone to teach her gift to.

She set the mail on the table just inside the door, where William would deal with it, and headed for the kitchen, both to see how Olga was getting on and possibly grab a snack. But as she was walking away, the gate intercom buzzed, so she turned back.

The screen beside the door showed a man who'd apparently come out for a run, in shorts, t-shirt from a local Irish pub, and sweatband. Marissa pressed the "speak" button. "What's up?"

The man raised a hand, showing a croquet ball. *"I just found this in my yard. Thought you might want it back? You know, it's bad to break up the set."* He grinned.

If this was the next-door neighbor, he might already be familiar with all the members of the household. Or, he might only know the human ones. Better to be safe. She pressed a button that rang bells all over the property to warn of a mundane visitor, then the button to open the gate. Everyone who needed to, knew to get out of sight quickly, and anyone who couldn't hear wore a buzzer.

Marissa waited on the steps as the neighbor walked up the drive. He was very tall, very skinny, maybe sixty years old but fit, with tousled, caramel-colored hair. When he got close, he tossed her the ball, then transferred a stack of mail from his other hand, to offer that hand.

Marissa shook it, briefly. "Thanks."

"No problem! You know, I moved in a couple weeks ago, and I've been meaning to say hi. I'm Rex, by the way. Rex Edmunds. Nice spread you've got here."

"It's not mine—this is Priscilla Wheelwright's house. I'm just a…." They hadn't discussed what she should tell people about herself. "…a friend."

"May I meet the lady of the house?"

"Um, she keeps odd hours, so I'm not sure if she's ready for company. I just got here myself, but I could check."

"If it's convenient. I can come back some other time—I just think it's important for neighbors to know each other."

"Sure. Why don't you come in?"

Leaving him to look at the engravings on the wall of the foyer, she went back to look for anyone who could deal with the visitor. She didn't have to look long—William met her halfway down the great hall. "What's going on, miss?"

"The next-door neighbor dropped in to see Ms. Wheelwright. Is she available?"

The old butler scowled at her. "You let him in?"

"I pressed the alert button first. Isn't that okay?"

"Young lady." William drew a breath. "Everyone who needs to, has hidden themselves, but have a little consideration. They all have things to do, and it's inconvenient for them to drop everything on a moment's notice just because you feel like inviting someone in."

"Ah. Okay, sorry. I just thought we shouldn't look like we have something to hide."

"Nobody expects wealthy people to see every random stranger who drops by." William walked past her toward the front door. "Go to the conservatory—Ms. Wheelwright is expecting you."

She found Ms. Wheelwright kneeling over one of the planters. She looked up from packing dirt around the base of a palm tree. "Any luck with the mail?"

"Sorry."

"Hmph." Ms. Wheelwright stood, brushing her gloved hands together, then took off the gloves to lay them tidily over the edge of the planter. "Well, perhaps we need to modify our approach."

"Or maybe I just can't do it."

"I still believe you have the gift—I definitely feel something there. Just let me think about it. What was the alarm about?"

"You have a visitor. Sorry about that. William already told me I shouldn't have let him in."

"Who is it?"

"Your neighbor one house to the south."

"Mister Paluzzi?"

"Er, no, he said Edmunds. He's new."

"I do hope nothing's happened to dear Mister Paluzzi. I'll have to inquire. But I may not want to talk with him long. Would you please return in five minutes with an excuse to allow me to escape the conversation if I choose?"

"You want me to lie?"

"Yes. Rather than my telling him, 'I'm bored, please go away.'"

Marissa grinned. "Okay. I'll go check on Olga."

She found Olga in the kitchen, on a barstool at the counter, chopping onions. The Goloopa was also there, braids limp from steam, stirring two pots on the large range while their tail held a cookbook open. Marissa waved and leaned against the counter near Olga. "Hey! You already started the new job?"

"Nah." Olga scraped the board into a bowl, wiped her eyes on her sleeve, and reached for another onion. "I just happened to be here and felt like cutting up fifteen pounds of vegetables for fun. I was getting the lowdown on how they do things here, but there was an alarm or something and everybody ran hide, so there was nobody else to help with the cooking."

Oops. "What about...?" Marissa nodded at the Goloopa. "Why didn't they hide?"

"I don't know. It doesn't explain anything, just tells me what to do."

The Goloopa was scowling at them, or maybe that was just "resting creature face." "What you do in my kitchen?" they boomed.

"Staying out of the way for a few minutes."

The Goloopa tossed its head, braids flying. "You not out of *my* way. You got few minute, you grate cheese."

Every meal was a production in this house, with several different types of mouth to feed, so most of this must be lunch, but it looked like they'd also gotten an early start on dinner. Some of the things they were preparing smelled intriguing, others... not. Marissa opened the oversized fridge. There were several packages on the cheese shelf.

The Goloopa came over and touched a box. "Medium cheddar, coarse." Pointed at a cabinet. "Grater there." Walking back to the stove, they paused, ears swiveling toward the hallway door, tensing. "Someone comes." They started toward the other door, then paused again, relaxed, and grinned, revealing long yellow teeth. The grin was possibly even more disconcerting than the scowl.

The hall door swung open, and a stranger came through. Like Mr. Edmunds from next door, this man was tall and thin. Unlike Mr. Edmunds, he was burnt brown and leathery, with a ponytail of long, sun-bleached hair, a frayed t-shirt, and stained jeans that looked faded from hard use rather than having been sold that way. He saw the Goloopa, smiled, and said "He-e-e-y," advancing with open arms.

Marissa resisted the urge to shout a warning as the Goloopa lurched for him, arms encircling him, smooshing his face into their chest. "Spider!" they said.

Olga was also watching with interest and raised an eyebrow at Marissa. Marissa shrugged. It was the first time she'd seen the Goloopa act anything less than annoyed.

Spider disengaged from the enthusiastic hug, patted the Goloopa's arm, and looked around the room. "You folks are new."

"Olga." The Goloopa pointed. "Marissa."

"Oh!" Spider looked at her with interest. "This is 'The One?'"

Marissa grimaced. "So they say. Ms. W doesn't seem sure, but she thinks I can probably do it, so I'm in training to eventually replace her."

He turned to Olga. "And you?"

"I'm a replacement, too. I'm replacing Marie." Olga waved her knife genially and got back to chopping.

The Goloopa, still smiling in that disturbing way, returned to the stove. Spider wandered over to where Marissa was working. "Need help?"

She pointed at the Goloopa. "Ask."

He returned in a minute with a mortar and pestle and a measuring cup full of orange grains. He poured some grain into the mortar and started grinding. "Now that she's found you, is Priscilla still testing every new person she meets?"

At their first meeting, Ms. W had touched Marissa's forehead, delivering a jolt of dizzy, before declaring her the chosen one. "I don't think so. But based on my performance so far, maybe she should keep looking."

"Give it time, you'll get better. You're a friend of Ruby's, right?"

"You know her?"

"We've met. She's kind of a force of nature."

She dumped grated cheese into a bowl to make room in the grater. "Yeah. She hasn't mentioned you, though."

"We were ships in the night. Passing, we mocked each other briefly, were united in our disdain for The Man, then went our separate ways, both improved." He turned to look at the Goloopa. "Hey bud, can I have an apple?"

"Sure."

He reached to take one from a large wooden bowl and took a bite before going back to his grinding. "Apple," he muttered. "Pal. Alp. Pale." He took another bite. "Lap."

Realizing what he was doing, Marissa added, "Plea. Peal."

"No, there's only one 'e'—oh, right, with an 'a.'" He laughed. "Sorry. I got this game on my phone and got a little obsessed. Can't hear a word anymore without thinking what other words I can make with those letters."

Marissa dumped the last of the cheese into the bowl and looked at the clock. Five minutes were almost up. "I've got to go, but it was nice to meet you."

He touched his brow in a casual salute. "Maybe I'll see you here at dinner tonight?"

"I guess you will." She left the grater near the sink and hurried back down the hall to the conservatory. She found Edmunds and Ms. W among the potted plants by the window wall, talking about thrips, whatever those were.

She stood, waiting to be officially noticed. Thrips. Hips. Rip. Stir. Spit.

Ms. W grabbed her cane and levered herself up from a seat on the edge of a giant plant pot. "What is it, dear?"

"Margo asks whether you called Bob yet. He's only in the office until noon."

"Ah. Thank you for the reminder. I haven't called yet." She turned to her guest. "Mister Edmunds—"

"Do please call me Rex."

"I'm sorry, but there's a matter of business I must attend to."

Edmunds waved a hand. "Oh, no problem. It's fortunate you had any time with me just dropping in like this. Let's continue our chat some other time."

"Quite. Marissa, will you show Mister Edmunds to the door?"

"Okay." She started walking, collecting Edmunds with a look as she passed.

He fell in beside her. "It's unusual to see friends of such different ages. As you and Priscilla, I mean. It's a fine thing."

She was quite certain Ms. W hadn't asked him to call her by her first name. "She's got lots of friends."

He looked around. "This is a fascinating house. The cat bridges and tunnels.… I'm more of a dog person myself, but such a wonderful idea. And the very eclectic art collection."

"She does it her way." They were just passing the stack of olive cans, which Marissa had never been sure was really supposed to be an artwork or just an example of Ms. W's weird sense of humor. She wouldn't be surprised to learn Ms. W had built it herself to see how many people would try to figure out its artistic meaning.

"I'm not living in the main house next door," Edmunds said. "I'm renting the coach-house while I work on a book."

"Oh? What's it about?" It wasn't likely to be anything interesting, but she couldn't just walk beside him in silence all the way to the gate.

"Education reform."

After her conversations with Olga, that actually was an interesting topic. "What are your ideas about that?"

"I don't know yet. That's why I have to write the book."

"Fair enough." Marissa opened the front door and ushered him out.

"I can find my way from here."

"I'm sure you can, but I'm supposed to lock the gate." That was untrue—the gate locked automatically. But it was more diplomatic than telling him she had to make sure he didn't wander on his own.

He looked around at the topiary lining the drive. "She certainly has skilled gardeners."

She'd never seen the gardeners at work, but from comments she'd overheard, they might be gnomes. "They do all right."

"Say, do you know a decent barber in the neighborhood?"

They were almost to the gate. Marissa angled off to work the switch. "I don't live around here, but I've heard there's a website called Google where you can look that sort of thing up."

He grinned and stood near the gate, waiting for it to open. "I've enjoyed meeting you, miss…?"

"Marissa."

He gave a tiny bow. "Until next time."

She waited for the gate to close, then walked back to the house.

So. Not so great at being The One. What with this and soccer and interrupting everyone's morning with the mundane alarm, not a red letter day so far.

She was excellent in school and thought she'd have no trouble learning tweaking, but it was so nebulous, and Ms. W kept telling her to "experiment" instead of giving clear instructions. Ms. W hadn't had a teacher and had to figure it all out for herself. Marissa couldn't imagine doing that. She clearly didn't have a natural gift for it, if she could even really do it at all.

And did she even want to? She'd always wanted to go to space. If she did master this future-manipulating trick, wouldn't she end up like Ms. W, a weird woman in the center of a web, tugging at the threads to prevent disasters, keeping secrets hidden and things running smoothly? She could hardly do that from Mars. Maybe it was just as well if she couldn't do it.

She found Ms. W still in the conservatory at the wrought-iron table in the middle of the room, sorting her mail. She looked up as Marissa approached and pushed one pile across the table toward her. "Look what William brought me."

The top piece on the pile was addressed to Arnold Paluzzi. They all were, in fact, or had "Current Resident" and the next-door address. "How did this get here?"

"You tell me."

"Oh, I know. Mister Edmunds had it in his hand when he came in. He must've set it down in the entry next to our mail and forgotten it when he left."

"The entry is called a foyer." Ms. W took the letters back and squared them up. "So, throwing the croquet ball into his yard actually did result in someone else's mail being delivered to us."

"Yes, but not by the letter carrier."

"The main goal was achieved. You need only work on precision."

"Really? Because this just seems like luck to me."

"When it works, it usually seems like chance. The connection between the result and what you did to cause it is rarely even as direct as in this case." Ms. W gestured with an envelope for emphasis. "I think the problem may be that I was too prescriptive. The style that works for me might not be best for you. I want you to find your own way. Perhaps you're less visual than I am and should try to bring in other senses. Perhaps instead of rods and gears, you should try, I don't know. Ripples in water. Or think of something else."

"So, I'm sorry, you're telling me you're going to be even less specific about how to do this?"

"Just"—Ms. W waved—"experiment."

When Ruby came home for lunch, Captain Urbana and Simon were in the study, standing over the desk, looking at papers, talking too softly to hear from the doorway. Simon scribbled something on a sheet and pushed it over to Urbana's side. She glanced at it, nodded, and made a note on a tablet.

They worked well together. Good friends, even though Urbana apparently would've let him rot in jail. To be fair, she might've had some plan Ruby didn't know about to get him out—it's not like Urbana would've told her. Besides, she and Simon had gone to high school together, fought the odd monster or two. She'd encouraged Simon to move to Chicago. Maybe they'd even been lovers—gross thought.

Simon looked up and saw her and glanced at the clock. "Time for lunch." He tidied the papers into a pile. "We'll finish this later. I didn't have time to cook, but there's deli stuff in the fridge. I'll eat later. I have a call scheduled with a supplier."

"Sure. Susan and I will talk in the kitchen." Ruby knew Urbana didn't like her to use her first name. She headed down the hall, leaving Urbana to follow. Ruby rummaged in the fridge. "Potato salad, pickled peppers, olives, um, cheese I can't pronounce, corned beef, turkey, mysterious reddish substance. What'll you have?"

Urbana took out plates and a box of cracker breads from the cupboard and seated herself at the counter. "Bring it all."

Ruby threw everything onto a tray. "So, I read your report about the Skohlars."

"There's a nice switch. If you read reports, you're already ahead of most of my coworkers."

"I spend a lot of time on trains, so I have time to read. So there are a bunch of things we're asking for, but I've been thinking about the two you mentioned before. They have to stop the monster fights and quit stealing things."

"I believe that's the only way the wider community will accept them."

"But you already stopped them from getting any more creatures to use in their fights."

Urbana glopped potato salad onto her plate. "We think we have. But when they run out, they might continue with dogs or roosters or something else they can get locally. Even if they only fight each other, it would be a perception problem, though I suppose we could settle for that, provided participation is voluntary. Will you have some, uh, reddish substance?"

"I'll serve myself, thanks. Then what about the stealing?"

"We don't expect to stop them, as you know. I hope to have Crunchy Bits O' Cheddar issue an edict to that effect."

Ruby tasted the reddish substance. Still not sure what it was, but it was tasty—a little tart, a little sweet. Some sort of fruit. "You want their chief to make a law he can't enforce."

"Try the red stuff on the cheese. Yes."

"Doesn't that undermine his authority?"

Urbana wiped potato salad from the corner of her mouth. "Not if he frames it right. We're fooling the stupid humans by agreeing to this to get what we want, but we won't really do it."

"Don't steal, wink wink."

"Precisely."

The red stuff was indeed very nice with cheese. "Okay. So why even bother?"

"To help keep it under the radar. If there are impossible crimes, like burglaries that only could happen if the burglars are tiny, the Cheddar will be forced to take action."

"So you really just want to prevent stuff that's hard to explain to the mundanes."

"As you well know, that's what I always want. This rule might cut into their income a little, but it'll make my job easier."

"Of course, if they quit buying monsters, and giant bags of Purina Monster Chow, they don't need as much money."

Urbana nodded. "I wish we knew why they insist on doing that. It's some cultural thing we don't get. It would be nice if they were more up front about what they want."

"There should be some way to find out more. What do you hear from, um, the rodent on the street?"

"Mph. Reach me another napkin, please? We don't hear anything because they won't let us send anyone down there to do like live rodent interviews."

Ruby went to the fridge for a soda. "Really? I know an anthropologist at the Field Museum who would just *love* to be the first to research them."

Urbana sat up straighter. "You will *not*—"

Ruby waved a hand. "I know, I know. I'm not an idiot. I'm just saying, if you want to understand them, it'd be nice to send someone who knows how to get them to let her in and what questions to ask. Doctor Rora has talked her way into a couple of really what's-the-word tribes. Reclusive."

"We'll take it under advisement."

Uncle Simon's house had several nonstandard features. A sometimes-attic, sometimes guest apartment was one. Another was the secret sub-basement. Half of that was fitted out as an exercise and practice space, with a mirror wall and padded floor. It was a good place to teach Kirk the basic forms.

"Peppy," Ruby said.

He shifted more or less smoothly into the next position, then spoiled it with a wobble. "Damn. You should go down there. To visit the Skohlars, I mean."

"Will you please focus?" She adjusted his arm. "Bend the right knee a little more."

"All I'm saying is, if they asked for you at the negotiations, maybe they would let you into their tunnels."

"I really shouldn't have told you about it. Left foot this much farther out and pointed more to the side."

Kirk shifted his foot.

"Eyes ahead." Ruby pushed his shoulder to test his balance. "Acceptable. And what's this position?"

"Peppy."

"Right. And this is khaki." Ruby stood beside him on the padded floor, watching their reflections in the mirror wall. She took the same posture, then slid back, twisting her body, warding with her forearm, other hand reaching out below. "Khaki."

Kirk copied her, wobbling again.

Ruby scrutinized the positions of his limbs. "This is actually kind of useful for me. Seeing your crappy form, I see why I'm supposed to stand in a particular way."

"So glad I can help."

"Keep your center of gravity lower."

"Easy for you to say, shorty."

"Just take a wider stance." She touched a spot with her toe. "Move your foot up here. Good. Now eppy."

They went back and forth between the two positions a few times. "Ok. Here's khaki again."

Kirk copied the movement. "Where does he get these names? What does he even call this martial art?"

"He calls it 'fighting.' He has his own way, but it seems to work. Ready? Faster now. Eppy, peppy, khaki."

"What's this combination for?"

"Come at me, and I'll show you."

She helped him up after the demonstration. "Anyway, I don't even know if I'd fit in their tunnels."

"They've had people in there to do work for them, right? And that Sasquatch got in with no problem. A lot of it must be human sized."

Ruby sighed. "Frankly, I'd be terrified to go. It's probably tight quarters in a lot of places, it's dark, and they're armed and unpredictable. Okay now, eppy. I'll come at you, slowly."

Going back upstairs afterward, they crowded together in the narrow elevator tube. The platform rose quietly, lifting them from the sub-basement to the basement of Simon's house, merging invisibly with the pattern of the tile floor.

"This is actually the coolest house ever." On the way to the stairs, Kirk paused near the holding cells to look at the long scratches on the cinderblock wall. "What did he keep in here?"

"And where are the bars to keep it locked in? I don't know, and he doesn't say. Come on, we don't want to be late for rehearsal. You can have the shower first."

While Kirk ran upstairs with his gym bag, Ruby grabbed the mail from the floor near the front door. Junk, junk, bill… hello, what was this? Something for her, a creased card envelope, addressed to her at Aunt Meg's address in block letters, scratched out and re-addressed in Aunt Meg's handwriting. Ruby hadn't even bothered to submit a forwarding form at the post office because who would be writing to her? From the postmark, Meg had apparently hung onto it for a week before sending it on. She sat on the stairs and ripped it open, taking out a small sheet of lined notebook paper.

Dear Ruby,

You helped me before. My ma is gone again, and they're planning to send me away to some other family. I don't know how to talk with these people, but I need to be here when she comes back. Don't let them take me away.

—Danno

"What the hell?" She turned the note over, but there was nothing on the back. Where had she left her phone? She ran upstairs, looked around, and flipped back the covers of her bed, finally finding the phone on the dresser, which technically was where it belonged. She dialed Aunt Meg's number and waited through three rings.

"*Hello?*"

"Gerard? It's Ruby. Let me talk to your mom."

"*Okay.*"

She read through the note again, but it contained no more information than it had before. Finally, there was sound from the other end. "*Hello?*"

"I have a letter here from Danno Farrugia. What's going on?"

"*That boy wrote to you? Why?*"

Ruby closed her eyes and counted to five. "Yes. It's what you forwarded to me."

"*Oh, that letter? Well, you should call the sheriff.*"

"What? Why?"

"*He's missing, last I heard.*"

Ruby bumped her forehead against the door frame. "He's missing, and you held onto his letter over a week before sending it on?"

"Young lady, I don't appreciate your tone. I didn't know who it was from, or I'd have taken it straight to the sheriff myself. What does it say?"

"Never mind what it says. How is he missing? Since when?"

"I don't follow the doings of those sorts of folks."

Those sorts of folks. "What happened to his mom?"

"She took off. He probably covered for her, so who knows how long she's been gone. Again, if it's not in the newspaper I wouldn't know. I suggest you call the sheriff."

There was a *click* from the other end.

"Hello?" Ruby looked at the phone. Call ended. "Fine." She looked up another number and dialed.

"Aitkin County Sheriff's Department, this is Jana."

Ruby moved the phone to her other ear. "I need to talk with someone about Danno Farrugia."

"I'm afraid we can't comment on ongoing investigations."

"I just got a letter from him."

There was a pause from the other end. *"Just a moment, please."* Hold music started playing.

Kirk showed up in her doorway in a t-shirt and jeans, hair wet from the shower. "Your turn."

"I need a minute."

"We'll be late."

"Then we'll be late." The hold music ended, and she held up a finger.

"Deputy Pete Forbes." In the background, there what sounded like an electric fan and radio noises. *"What can I do you for?"*

"Hey. Are you still looking for Danno Farrugia? I got a letter from him."

Pete instantly sounded more alert. *"Who is this?"*

"Ruby Park, calling from Chicago. I used to live in Aitkin, and that's how I know him."

"Would this be the same Ruby who chased—"

"Yes, yes." Ruby signaled Kirk, who was looking at her with

raised eyebrows, to wait. "That was me. Small town, you know—ha ha. Is he still missing?"

"We're still looking, yes. What does this letter say?"

"Do you have a place I can send you a picture of it? Yeah?" Ruby went to her desk to write down the information, then snapped a photo of the letter and envelope and forwarded it to him. "Okay, sent. He says his mother is missing. Is she okay? Has she turned up?"

"Not yet, but she's gone AWOL before, so we're not too concerned about her. Got your email, gimme a sec."

They weren't concerned about someone who'd been missing for well over a week?

"What's going on?" Kirk whispered. "Whose mom is missing?"

"A boy I know. He's got… challenges and can't take care of himself."

There was a scraping sound at the other end, like a phone being dragged across a desk. *"Well, this letter is pretty old."*

"Yeah, my aunt didn't forward it right away."

"Not much help, either. He ran away from the foster home where he was placed. Took clothes and food when he left. I don't suppose you have any idea where he'd go? Any places he likes to hide, people he'd run to?"

"When he's upset, he usually goes into the woods northeast of his house."

A pause on the line. *"Black's Wood? We've searched it."*

"If he wants to be close by so his mom can find him, that's where he'd be. He knows you'll find him if he goes home to wait, but he's probably checking now and then to see if she's back." If he was all right. But she wouldn't think that.

"We searched more than once." From the tone of voice, he wasn't eager to search again. *"And it's pretty far from the foster household."*

Seriously? "Look, Deputy Pete, you're a—do you consider yourself a big strong man?"

"What are you getting at?"

"There are no such things as ghosts. If you search the woods carefully, you'll find him." One way or another. "Look, his brain is different, but he's not stupid. He can find his way home, so he'll be somewhere near there."

"Miss Park, thank you for the information. If I need to talk with you again, can I use this same number you're calling from?"

"Yes. What happens if you do find him and his mom is back? Would you still send him back to foster care?"

"I can't comment on that."

Ruby thought she could guess. Annie Farrugia was an alcoholic and didn't take great care of Danno at the best of times. If she'd left again without a really excellent reason, it wasn't likely she'd get her son back.

"We'd very much like to talk with her, of course, so if you hear from either of them, we'd appreciate a call. You can ask for extension thirty-four."

Ruby jotted it down. "Will you call me if you find either of them?"

"It'll be in the paper."

She didn't get the Aitkin local paper, of course, but presumably they had a website. "Fine." She hung up.

Kirk had seated himself on her bed to wait. "Did I understand correctly that the missing boy is hiding out in a haunted forest?"

"Everybody in town thinks there's weird stuff going on there, and admittedly it's dark and kind of creepy, but it's just a forest. I can't believe the Sheriff's Deputies are such cowards, though."

Kirk shrugged. "Then if you're right, they'll look, and find him."

"Yeah, I'm not sure they'll look." Ruby checked the time on her phone. "We'd best get going. I'll make the shower quick and meet you at the car."

They were quiet on the way to Marissa's place, Ruby busy worrying about Danno and Kirk thinking whatever he was thinking. They stopped at a light, and she caught him glancing at her. "What? You look like you want to say something."

The light changed, and Kirk drove on. "How do you know the woods aren't haunted?"

"Duh, because ghosts aren't real?"

"Marissa said you said your guitar is haunted."

"I didn't mean it. I've just been having weird dreams. People make up ghosts in their own heads."

"I bet a few months ago you'd've said Sasquatches aren't real."

"So I should just believe anything now? I was wrong about one thing, so I should give up using my brain to determine what's true?"

"You wanted to know what was on my mind. That was it."

Ruby looked out the window at the passing buildings. "All right. Sorry. I've been there, and there were no spooks." She looked at him again. "I have to go look for him."

He glanced at her, then back at the road. "You mean to go to Minnesota? You think you'll find him when the police couldn't?"

"I have to try."

Three

It took a train and two buses to get to Ms. Wheelwright's neighborhood. Ruby waited ten minutes at the stop. Marissa flashed her a grin as she hopped off her bus, arms outstretched, then paused. "What's the matter?"

Ruby moved in for a hug. "A friend is in trouble." While they walked, she told Marissa about the Danno situation, giving her the letter to read.

Marissa looked it over. "He's your friend? How old is he? This looks like it was written by a little kid."

"He's sixteen, but he's got challenges. He's really much smarter than he comes across."

Marissa handed the letter back. "Well, this really sucks. Now I'll worry about him, too. I guess all we can do is hope, though."

Ruby paused to look into the window of a pet store. "Oh, I don't think I'll just stay home hoping."

"What, then? You're going out there?"

"If I can. I'll ask Simon. If I just said I wanted to visit Aunt Meg's family, he'd let me go. I mean, he'd be incredulous, but he'd still do it."

"You're going to lie to him?"

"No, I'm just saying I have enough excuse to go anyway. I don't see why he'd be fussed if I looked around in the woods, too. I can't get lost with GPS." Ruby leaned against the pet store window, shading her eyes to look inside.

"He might let you go to Minnesota, but I think we've already established that Simon isn't going to let you get a cat."

"Shut up. A girl can dream. Anyway, if I do well with the thing I'm not supposed to tell you about, he'll owe me bigtime. Not the Danno thing. Something else."

When they got to Ms. W's house, Marissa let them into the gate. "Mind if we walk around the side?"

"I'd like it. I've never seen the gardens." Ruby settled her backpack more securely, and they followed a meandering gravel path around the house, past a little pond, a large dome of colorful pottery labeled "gnome den," which probably wasn't merely decorative, through a circular rose garden, past fenced vegetables planted in neat rows, and into the formal English garden Ruby had already seen from inside the conservatory. There was a group of people on the patio there, mostly familiar but not all expected.

Netta Polacek, widow of Simon's late colleague, dressed in a drab pantsuit, smiled wanly as they walked up. Spider Terboositer gave her a goofy grin and a peace sign. Police Detective Derek Garbers, the only person they'd been able to show the invisible monster they'd slain before the Skohlars melted the remains. Dr. Sin, who gave Ruby a grave salute with his highball glass. A sweaty, middle-aged man in a poorly-fitting suit, who'd come with Ms. W to Polacek's funeral, though she hadn't gotten his name. Ruby pointed. "Who's that?"

"Terrence Underwood, Ms. W's nephew."

"And the woman in blue?"

"That's Margo, her secretary."

"Okay, I've spoken to her on the phone a couple times." By this time, they were getting within earshot of the party. "Mister Terboosit-er." She held out her fist for a bump from Spider. "I didn't know you were back in town. What have you been doing with yourself?"

"Oh, little of this, little of that." He brushed long, loose hairs back from his face. "Went to a folk music festival in Toronto. Did a bit of fence fixing in Wyoming. Searched for mountain fairies in Utah."

"Fairies."

"Didn't find any, though. Might be extinct. Habitat loss."

Marissa had paused to greet Netta, but she looked over at this. "What would you do if you found some?"

"Oh, the usual. Count 'em, and if they'll talk, find out if they need anything. And then I got a contract to transport some… well, it's a big hairy deal, anyway, so here I am."

Ruby waved a hand in front of his face. "Hang on, though. I want to know about this fairy census. Did someone pay you to do this?"

"A little bit. I had a grant from the ICDF. I'm crap at paperwork, but there's a poet in Tucson who sends in applications for me, for a little commission. I think she mostly just believes in that kind of work, you know?"

"ICDF?"

Spider took out a pack of cigarettes and shook one loose. "Short for International Cryptid Defense Fund, something like that."

"How long does it generally take to get these grants?"

"Oh, I don't know. Mary just tells me when one comes in. A few months, maybe?"

Netta joined their circle. "Hey, Ruby. Are you talking about cryptid survey work? Alasdair used to do that sometimes to pick up the slack when business was slow. Give me your email address, and I'll send you information. The pay's not great, though, and they want people with a little field experience."

"Ruby's a naturalist," Marissa said. "The first time she told me that, I thought it meant she went around in the nude, but apparently not."

Ruby shot her a look. "I've done frog and bird census. But I'm heading somewhere soon, so I was hoping for a quick answer."

"Sometimes Alasdair would go ahead and do the work before the money came through. If it's a place that's way overdue for a visit, they always approve it."

"What if it's a supposedly haunted forest?"

"Maybe. You'd have to check the website." Netta took out her phone and made a note. "Someone has to refer you to get an account, but I can do that."

"Excellent! Thanks!"

Spider waved the cigarette, which he'd been holding, unlit. "'Scuse me, folks, I just wanna…." He retired into the distance.

Ruby turned back to Netta. "I've been wanting to talk with you. I haven't seen you since the memorial service. How are you doing?"

"Well, crappy, but that's to be expected."

"Yeah. Simon sends his regards and invites you to visit."

Netta nodded. "Thanks."

"He's crazy busy with all your husband's clients as well as his own. Are you sure you don't want to keep the business going? He'd send those clients right back to you."

Netta waved this away. "I just don't do that. Anyway, I have to stay home for Ray."

"How's he doing? I hope he's not still blaming the Skohlars."

Netta's lips thinned. "No, we know it wasn't their fault. That Sasquatch was responsible. Look, actually there's something I need to talk with Reggie about. Talk later?"

When she'd gone, Marissa pulled Ruby aside. "Fairies?"

"First I've heard of them. But if I can get these guys—the ICDF, was it—to pay me for something I planned on doing, anyway…." Ruby shrugged.

A bell rang, and everyone turned to look. William stood on the patio, wearing a sharp-looking black suit. He rang the bell again, and people stopped talking. "The meal is about to commence. Please come in and take your seats."

Everyone filed in after him through the conservatory and down a short hall to the dining room. The table could have accommodated three times the number present, and all the place settings were down at one end. Ruby sat farthest from the head of the table. Marissa sat beside her and Spider across from them.

Detective Garbers sat next to Spider, holding out his hand. "I don't believe we've met. Derek Garbers."

Spider looked up at him, hesitating to take his hand. Ruby gave him a warning look, and he grinned and shook the detective's hand. "Hey, man. I'm Spider. You're new to The Scene, then?"

Ruby spoke up. "He was helpful in that recent business with…" Did everyone at this table already know about the Skohlars? "…with the monster. I guess it's been a wild couple of months for you, since then, Detective?"

Derek flapped his napkin and set it in his lap. "I've learned a lot. The Guardians need more people and especially folks in law enforcement. So, I've been fielding a lot of calls. Not, fortunately, homicides, at least so far."

Marissa leaned in. "You signed up with the Guardians? How does that work? I mean, if an officer arrests someone… odd? How do you get involved? What do you tell them?"

"That doesn't happen often, fortunately. The ones who are too strange to pass as human, those mostly stay out of sight. If it looks like someone will make trouble—some human, I mean—there's something they, or rather we, can do to make them forget the last few hours, but I don't know any cases of it being used."

Olga, dressed in a maid's uniform, entered with a large tray of covered plates. She reached over Dr. Sin's shoulder to set one before him. He leaned out of the way and joined their conversation. "Memory erasure really is a last resort. Besides being expensive, the subject is likely to try to account for the missing time, and that can cause as much trouble as their just knowing what happened. If we confiscate all the evidence, that's generally enough. Tabloids might still run the story, but that's not a problem since nobody believes them."

Olga set a plate in front of Spider, then walked the long way around the end of the table to give one to Ruby, who immediately looked under the silver dome.

Marissa tried to peek. "What is that?"

"Not food." Ruby lifted the cover and took out a flat package a little larger than her hand, wrapped in newspaper and tied with a ribbon. "I didn't know there were going to be presents. Didn't buy her anything."

"I'm not expecting any, Miss Park." Ms. W pulled out her chair at the head of the table with a scrape. "Please, open your packages now. Olga, you may bring out the salad."

Ruby pulled at the ribbon and tore the newspaper to reveal a flat box that made her think of jewelry. A necklace? But no, when she opened the cover, she found a small wooden frame hung with silver bells resting on crushed velvet beside a wooden-handled knocker. She looked over to see what Marissa had gotten. Hers had come in a jewelry case also, and hers was actually jewelry of a sort—a ring of two metal bands of letters and symbols on a black background between three narrower stripes of silver.

Marissa put it on. "It's a decoder ring." She twisted one of the black bands, which moved smoothly with quiet, expensive-sounding clicks. "Very nice. Thank you!"

Ms. W nodded. "I suggest you all keep these items on your persons until you need them."

Netta turned her gift over in her hands. "Is this a taser? I hope I won't need it."

"Nothing is ever certain, dear. If you don't require it in the next month, I don't expect you will. Take care, now—it's charged."

Netta shrugged and tucked the device away in her purse.

"What do you have?" Marissa whispered. "Bells?"

Ruby turned the box to face her. "They're more your thing I'd've thought. Percussion, right?"

Olga came out with a tray of salads. She set one in front of Spider, who stopped playing with the tiny pocketknife he'd unwrapped to examine the contents of his plate. "Pears."

"Spare," Marissa said. "Reaps."

"Ears," he replied, then after a pause, "apse."

"Good one. Um, sear."

"P-a-r-e-s."

Ruby picked up her fork—starting with the one on the outside, as Simon had recently taught her. "What the hell are you two doing?"

"Just a little game." Marissa took a sip of water. "What did you get, Detective?"

Derek held up a wallet-size metal card containing an assortment of little tools. "It appears to be a lock picking kit."

"Is that even legal?"

"Not for you. It is for me, however." The detective pulled his wallet out and tucked the card into it. He lowered his voice. "Is this lady for real? I've heard she can predict the future or something."

Ruby looked at Marissa. If she didn't mention her tweaker training, Ruby certainly wasn't going to. "Simon thinks she's full of baloney, but she seems to get results."

Salad wasn't generally Ruby's thing, but this one was nice, dressed with a thick fruity vinegar, and the greens were fresh—possibly from the vegetable beds they'd passed on the way in. She didn't talk much, listening to the others at the table instead.

Derek leaned toward Dr. Sin. "You're from Malaysia, aren't you? Do you have relatives there? This Malay Flu that's been in the news…."

Dr. Sin dabbed at his lips with his napkin. "I'm from Singapore. I wish you wouldn't call it that. It's not necessarily from there originally, and there are cases now in India, southern Europe, and California. It's a worldwide problem, or it will be before long. But no, nobody in my family is in particular danger. The Malaysian and Singaporean governments took prompt action to contain the problem. Unlike your own government, I might add."

"You don't think it would be an overreaction to shut down the ports like they're talking about?"

"I do not."

Spider wasn't saying much. Ruby motioned him closer. "I want to know more about Micah."

"Remind me who that is."

"Deceased rock musician, friend of Simon's."

"Oh, okay. I know who you mean now. You might better talk to Simon, though—I didn't know him all that well."

"Nobody talks about him. I get the sense there's some mystery about how he died." She jumped a little as a hand passed in front of her face—Olga, removing her salad plate, then replacing it with a bowl of soup. "Thanks."

"He fell and broke his neck. I do recall some controversy about it, but you know how it is… they couldn't exactly send him in for an autopsy, so there was nothing proven and no suggestion of motive." Spider shrugged. "I was out of town, so I probably didn't hear all the details, plus it's been a while."

Ms. W's voice piped up. "Olga, dear, a moment, please."

Olga paused in the doorway, turning halfway around with a tray of salad plates.

"This soup is very bitter. Will you please ask cook about it?"

Dr. Sin held his spoon to his nose, sniffed, then tasted. "It seems fine to me. German snail, isn't it?"

Snail? Ruby stared at the spoonful she'd been about to eat, then set it back in the bowl.

"I think it's very tasty," Terrence said, taking a bite of his.

"Very well," Ms. W said. "Perhaps it's just me. It's not terrible, just not what I expected. You may bring in the blargh course in eight minutes. Anyway, you were saying about the Indian print collection…?"

Marissa had set her spoon down also, and Derek tasted his tentatively, but Spider dug in with apparent enjoyment. He looked at Ruby with a raised eyebrow.

"I'm saving room for blargh," she said. "I've heard it's good but never got to try it."

"I think you'll like it. They tell me you're Simon's apprentice now. What's that like?"

Ruby talked about her lessons while her soup cooled, and in a few minutes, Olga returned, this time with a tray filled with little dishes of brown lumps. She set the first in front of Ms. W, who was looking a little green.

Terrence reached out to touch her hand. "Auntie, are you all right?"

"I'm a bit dizzy, and my head hurts. Is there something wrong with the lights?"

Dr. Sin stood, and Netta pushed her chair back to get out of his way. He took Ms. W's wrist, and with his other hand tilted her head back to get light on her face. "Your pulse is very rapid. Is there some medication you should take for this?"

"Nonsense." Ms. W stood, swaying. "I'm healthy as a ho-houth." Her hand raised to her chest. "Oh!" She sat back down and began to slide to the floor. Terrence and Dr. Sin each grabbed an arm, keeping her upright as her eyes rolled back and her head drooped to the side.

"Someone call 9-1-1," Dr. Sin snapped. "She's having a stroke."

"On it!" Olga set the tray on the floor and ran out of the room.

Netta was hovering behind Ms. W's chair, hands fluttering. "What should we do for her?"

Derek also stood, moving toward the head of the table. "Nothing. If it's a stroke, there's nothing we can safely do." He poked a finger in Ms. W's soup bowl, licked it, and made a face. "Nobody eat another bite. Her soup tastes different than mine."

Terrence had gone pale. "Are you s-saying she's been poisoned?"

"I'm saying her soup is different. Everyone back away from the table. If anyone else feels unwell, or if anything tasted bitter, please speak up at once." His eyes roved over the room. "Nobody will be leaving this house for the present, and in fact, I'd like you all to stay right here in this room." Derek took out his phone. "I'm calling this in."

All the guests and household members—at least, the ones the police were allowed to know about—were eventually herded into Ms. W's parlor and watched over by a couple of uniformed cops. When Simon showed up, Ruby waved him over. He wove his way through the crowd and sat beside her on the window seat. "Well." He adjusted his tie. "Another interesting evening. The police wouldn't tell me anything on the phone, but from what I overheard here, I gather Ms. Wheelwright has been poisoned."

"Seems so. And by the way, don't say 'Funny she didn't see it coming' because Marissa already chewed me out for that. She's very upset. Everyone here loves the old bat, and they're all worried."

"I wouldn't dream of saying any such thing."

"No, but I could see you thinking it. You get this little crooked grin when you've thought of a joke you're holding back."

The little grin vanished. "Do I? Well, you have a 'tell' too—you actually say it."

"I'm working on my diplomatic skills, I'll have you know, though admittedly I could've done better tonight. Anyway, Marissa says the power doesn't work well on things that affect themselves. The more something involves them directly, the more it fuzzes out. It's a paradox thing, I think."

"A sort of nearsightedness."

"Right." Ruby leaned to look around Derek's partner, a short, heavy-set man who blocked her view of Marissa. Her father stood talking to her, while she sat, red-eyed, saying nothing. It would be nice if she could do something to get him to lay off, but everything she could think of would only make matters worse. "They want to interview me, and I wanted you here. It hasn't been so long since I talked to these same cops about the last murder, you know?"

Simon twisted to look out the front window at the cars parked on the gravel. "I called Stefon, but it'll take time for him to get here."

"Who's Stefon? Oh, your lawyer? We don't need him. I just want to get it over with and go home."

"We can start talking to them when they're ready and see what they ask. If I say to stop and wait for him, though, you stop. Got it?"

"Got it."

It was half an hour more before Derek's partner poked his head in the door and beckoned to her. The lawyer hadn't arrived, so the two of them followed him through the hall to the library. He pointed them to seats around the round, leather-topped table in the middle of the room. "I'm Detective-Sergeant Bill Oscher."

Simon sat, crossing his legs. "We remember you."

The detective gave them a cool look. "I remember you two, too. Smack dab in the middle of trouble once more, are we?"

"We're not troublemakers," Simon said. "We're trouble finders. Or rather, it finds us."

"No doubt." Oscher pulled out a little blue notebook and a pen. "Let's get right down to it, shall we? Now then, Miss Park—"

"Hang on," Simon said. "Aren't you Detective Garbers's partner? Won't he be joining us?"

Oscher gave him a sour look. "He will not. And I'll ask the questions. Miss Park, would you please sketch out the seating arrangements at tonight's dinner?"

"Sure." Ruby took the notebook and drew the end of the table, filling in names at each position, then added a few more shapes and labels.

Oscher took the notebook back. "Well, the flower in the center is very pretty, but—"

"That represents the centerpiece, which partially blocked my view of Mrs. Polacek and Doctor Sin. Marissa mostly blocked my view of Margo and what's-his-name, the nephew. I assume you're going to ask whether any of them could've put anything into Ms. W's—I mean Wheelwright's—soup."

Oscher flipped to the next notebook page. "You seem very experienced with police interviews."

"I read a lot of mysteries. Anyway, I didn't see anyone reaching for her bowl, but we had our own conversation going at our end, so I probably wouldn't've noticed. Those three were all within reach of it."

"Please wait to answer the questions until I ask them. Let's take it from the top. Were there filled water glasses already on the table when you entered the room?"

This went on for several minutes before a uniformed officer came into the room and took Oscher aside for a whispered conversation. The detective returned and looked down at them. "Might either of you know where the cook can be found? Glooper, something like that."

Simon shrugged. "I never come here, so I'm not familiar with the staff."

They obviously weren't going to talk with the regular police. "The Goloopa is very shy," Ruby said. "I'm pretty sure they'd talk with Derek, though."

"First, if we can't find her, it doesn't matter who we have do the interview. Second, Detective Garbers isn't on this investigation, since everyone present is a suspect until they're ruled out."

Ruby sat up. "Wow. You think *he* might've poisoned the soup? I don't see how he could."

"We haven't established that *anyone* poisoned anything. We just have our procedures, and one of them... never mind. Please just tell me where she is if you know."

"They're a they, not a she. I don't know, but I bet someone here could find them if you had the right person to do the interview. If you won't let Derek, then how about Captain Urbana?"

Oscher gave a little snort. "I don't understand why you people try to drag her into everything. This isn't her department. Plus, the subjects of an inquiry don't get to choose who interviews them. We need to find the cook, and if sh—they flee, we'll treat that as highly suspicious."

Ruby spread her hands. "I'm just telling you how it is."

"We'll find her." Oscher sat and consulted his notes. "Now, what do you know about the person who was serving the meal? Olga."

Once Oscher reluctantly agreed they could go, they returned to the parlor to wait for their ride. Was this a good time to bring up the Minnesota thing? On one hand, Simon was mightily annoyed at getting dragged out for this. On the other hand, he had to realize that wasn't her fault, and time was short. She tried for a casual tone. "Hey, Unc, I need to go to Aunt Meg's."

"You have to go to Minnesota?" Simon gave her a skeptical look. "Why? When? For how long?"

"A friend is in trouble—it's urgent. Tomorrow morning there's an early bus. It's just for a few days. The mean detective didn't say not to leave town or anything."

"But we're supposed to meet with—" Simon paused and glanced around the parlor—no one was close enough to overhear. "You know. On Saturday."

"I'll be back by then."

Simon reached up as if he might plunge his fingers into his hair but dropped them again, leaving the hairs still perfectly arranged. "You can't believe how busy I am. I can't take you to Minnesota. I don't even have time to cook or do house repairs."

"You don't have to do a thing except pay the bus fare. Two hundred ought to cover it."

"You can't go on your own."

"Why not? I came here on my own."

Simon shut his eyes and raised his face to the heavens. "You couldn't just talk to your friend on the phone or something?"

"Since he's missing and everyone's looking for him—or failing to look, is the sense I get—no."

"And you think you can find him."

"I'm sure going to try."

Simon's phone buzzed, and he pulled it out. "Three minutes until our ride's here."

"All right, I'll meet you outside." Ruby had spotted Marissa and her dad coming back into the room, so she wove through the remaining crowd to pull her aside. "We're about to leave. Are you doing okay?"

Marissa sniffled. "Not really. It's all so horrible."

"Come here." Ruby pulled her friend into a long hug. "She might still be all right."

Marissa squeezed back, then pulled Ruby away from where her father was practicing his unhappy face. "It's not just Ms. W. They asked a lot of questions about Olga—how did she get the job, did I know she was in a gang, that sort of thing."

"*That* was quick. I mean, them finding out about the gang. I guess they already had a file on her."

Marissa lowered her voice. "They think it's suspicious, you know? I mean, her first day here, and this happens. And of course she could've easily put something in the soup without anyone seeing and made sure who got that bowl."

"She didn't, though. I mean, we don't know her *that* well, but she doesn't seem like the type. And Ms. W's going to do her a lot of good."

"I don't think it was her, but it had to be someone, and there's nobody here I'd want it to be."

She took Marissa's hands. "Maybe not. Maybe she just had a stroke. That would still be awful, but at least it's nobody's fault."

"Derek seemed pretty sure there was something in the soup, but yeah, we can hope."

A car horn sounded outside, and Ruby glanced at the window. "Look, I gotta go. Call me when you get home, okay?"

Ruby hopped into the car and slammed the door. Their driver had a Rasta hat and a fake Caribbean accent and was playing hip-hop on the radio. As he carefully crunched over the gravel around police vehicles still parked in the drive, Simon leaned over the seat. "Would you mind turning it down, just in back?"

This accomplished, he turned to Ruby, leaning in close so they could talk without being overheard. "I need you to explain the whole thing to me in detail."

"You were there—I told the police everything I know. Apart from, you know. Incidentally, whatever happened to your lawyer?"

"I texted him never mind since the interview was over anyway. But I meant explain to me about Minnesota."

"Oh." Ruby pulled out Danno's letter and repeated what she knew.

Simon used his phone as a flashlight to examine the letter and envelope. "How did they even know his mom was missing? Wouldn't he cover for her?"

"Danno's pretty much incapable of lying, so if I had to guess, I'd say no, he wouldn't if they asked him directly."

"And the woods near his house. That would be Black's Wood?"

"You know it?"

Simon nodded. "We lived in the house Meg lives in now until I was fifteen or so. The wood isn't haunted."

"Of course not."

"But there are fairies, or at least there were when I was a kid. If people still think the place is creepy, it's a good bet there are at least a few left."

"Good, then maybe the ICDF will pay for the trip." Ruby felt proud of being able to casually mention this, as if it were something she'd known all along rather than having just found out about it.

Simon failed to take any special note of her triumph, however. "More to the point, it means your friend isn't hiding out there unless the fairies are allowing it. And in that case, nobody will find him until he's ready to be found."

"You have an idea how to do that?"

Simon slipped the letter back into the envelope and tapped it against his knuckles. "Maybe. I'll tell you what, though."

"What?"

"This makes it legitimate business for the Agency. The fairies won't like policemen trampling through their wood. If we can help out, they'll owe us a favor."

"So you'll let me go?"

"Yes. But not by bus. Too slow. Let's see what a plane ticket costs."

Four

The airport in Brainerd, Minnesota, was tiny—just a few gates—but it still had the soulless feel of every airport ever. While Aunt Meg finished the paperwork at the gate, the agent snipped the unaccompanied minor tracking bracelet off Ruby's wrist.

"All set?" Aunt Meg gave her a critical once-over. "Not leaving anything behind? No checked bags?"

Ruby took another look around, hoping Speck would finally show up. Early in the flight, he'd left his tube and hadn't been seen since. If he'd gone wisp and passed through the wall of the plane, he'd've been left behind in an instant. Based on her testing, his top speed was about thirty mph, far slower than an airplane.

Well, there was nothing to be gained by worrying. He was okay. Probably. And if he could find her in Minnesota, he could find her just as easily in Aitken as at the airport. Ruby settled her backpack more comfortably on her shoulders. "I'm all set."

Meg walked away, leaving Ruby to follow. "I must say, it was very inconsiderate of Simon to not bring you himself. Expect me to drop everything at a moment's notice and wait hours at the airport. I hope you weren't expecting anything fancy for dinner because I haven't had a moment to do anything else today. Probably just order pizza."

Ruby had to hurry to keep up. "Thank you so much. Pizza is fine. Sorry to impose, but I really do think I can help find Danno."

"Let's hope it's not a wasted effort. Still, the boys will be glad to see you, I suppose."

The boys would not be glad to see her. She would not be glad to see the boys. But if their memories were good enough to recall why they shouldn't mess with her, they should get along okay.

Once on the road, Aunt Meg tuned the radio to a station where people were calling in to complain about liberals. Meg glanced over at her—evaluating her clothes? Seeing whether she'd gained weight? Who could say? She pulled her Cherokee onto a state highway and accelerated to a careful seven miles per hour over the speed limit. "How's Simon's business doing? He never calls me."

Ruby couldn't imagine why. "He's pretty busy."

"He always seems to be busy. I wasn't sure how well he'd do with a child to care for. You're keeping out of his hair, aren't you? Not being too much trouble?"

"I help out, actually."

"You help out doing investment counseling?"

Aunt Meg honestly believed Simon's cover story. A-mazing. "Obviously not, but there's a lot to do, running a business."

"That's true enough. Okay, then. If this arrangement is working out for both of you, maybe we should think about formalizing it. We can talk with your parents about making him your legal guardian instead of me."

Ruby had long been wanting that, but Simon hadn't brought it up. "That would probably be more convenient...."

"Right, no more trips to the notary for me, and what with school starting soon, it's not like I can pop on over every time you're called in to the principal's office." Meg laughed.

Ruby's jaw clenched. She looked out the window—flashes of water showing between the trees along the road.

Two months ago, she would've protested that she was never the one who started it. Back then, she'd had nobody on her side. Back then, she hadn't known she wasn't required to join every argument she was invited to. She closed her eyes and took a deep breath. "It's a good idea. You should ask Simon."

The rest of the ride was quiet, and her cousins were so busy with a new game system that they barely came out long enough to get their pizza. That was fine by Ruby, who hid out in the guest room with her book. She'd have liked to go straight to the woods, but it was only an hour to sunset.

There was a tentative knock on the door, and she looked over at it. The shadow of someone's feet was visible in the crack under the door. They began to move away, then returned. The knock was repeated.

Ruby set the book on the bed and got up to open the door. It was her cousin Charlie, age eight or nine—she forgot which. During her previous stay, she'd barely seen him, since he'd been away at a boarding school nearly the whole time.

"Hey." His voice was soft. "Can I come in?"

Ruby shrugged and returned to bed leaving the door open. Charlie closed it carefully behind him and sat on the end of the bed. "Whatcha reading?"

She showed him the cover. "It's about the Burgess Shale. Want to see some crazy critters?"

"Yeah."

She showed him some of the crazier ones, and he sat absorbed in the picture pages for a minute. Then he looked up at her. "Do you like it in Chicago?"

"I like it a lot."

"Can I go with you when you go back?"

What was this? "Why would you do that? Your family's here."

"They're going to send me back to Oak Hell. It's horrible."

Ruby set the book aside and considered him. It looked like he'd been crying. Nobody had explained to her why Charlie was in boarding school while his older brothers attended the local public school. "Can't you go back to school here?"

"Dad won't let me. They were mean to me at the school here, and I always got in trouble."

Tell me about it. "The boarding school isn't any better?"

"It's so much worse. All the meanest boys from all over the country get sent there." His lip began to quiver.

Ruby covered his hand with hers. "That sounds horrible. But you know I can't just take you back with me. That's up to your parents. You have to tell them how it is."

"I have told them. They think I'm just, just, I don't know a word."

"Being dramatic?"

"Yeah. The school never calls them when there's a problem. They just ignore it. I can't go back there."

Ruby rested her forehead on the heels of her hands. "Charlie, I'm really sorry. Let me think about it, but right now I don't see how I can help."

He looked at the floor and bumped his heels against the side of the bed. "Mom says you're here to look for Danno."

"Yeah."

"Can I come with for that, anyway? I like Danno."

"I have to go to the supposedly haunted wood, though."

Charlie scoffed. "The woods near his house? That's not haunted."

"I don't think so, either."

"There's leaf people, but they're nice."

Leaf. People. "Say what, now?"

"I only saw them a few times. They don't talk, but one time I was lost, and they led me back to the path."

"I see." Ruby stared at his profile. The kid had hidden depths.

He sighed and turned to look at her, sideways. "You don't believe me, either."

"No, no! Actually, I do believe you. And you're very welcome to come along."

Kirk's dad's welding shop was quiet, closed for the day. Marissa hauled the last of her drums out of the spare office and rolled it to the open space in the middle of the shop floor, beside where Kirk had set up a card table for the PC and camera.

"I'm just saying." Kirk took the tripod from its zipper bag and set it on the table. "Ruby's sub-basement is a much better band practice space than this. Hand me that camera, will you?"

Marissa held out the camera, and sighed. Kirk was awfully cute in his gangly, dorky way, but he had really stupid ideas. "My folks still don't like me to go over there. Dad refers to it as a House of Crime."

"But Simon was cleared of all charges."

"The best people, apparently, are never charged in the first place."

Kirk snorted. "Anyway, the sub-basement has pretty good acoustics. Padded walls."

"But Simon wouldn't let me leave my drums there, like your dad does, and I certainly can't bring them with me on the bus and haul them up and down stairs." She gestured around at the shadowy corners of the shop. "The sound might not be as good, but at least it's convenient."

"There's only one set of stairs—"

"And you're not taking my point. Before, I was going to suggest we ask Ms. W. She's got tons of space, and I'm over there all the time anyway. But I can't ask now, of course."

He adjusted the camera. "How's she doing?"

"Still unconscious. They don't give me medical details, but I think they're still calling it a stroke."

"Not poison, then?"

"Still poison. One of the detectives asked me a lot of questions about the soup today. They're very interested to talk with the cook, but the cook isn't human, so they're 'missing' until they send the right kind of detective."

He typed in his password. "Wally's not online yet." He swiveled. "But the cook can't control who gets which bowl of soup, right?"

"Unfortunately, they can in this case. Ms. W has a thing about never leaving any food on her plate, so she has them give her smaller servings so she doesn't overeat. I don't think the Goloopa poisoned her, but they could've done."

"So could anyone else who knew about her smaller servings, right? It didn't have to be someone sitting next to her."

"Yes, that does open it up. I think they might even suspect me. They asked if I knew the terms of her will."

Kirk glanced at the screen again. "Wow, do you think she might've left you something?"

"No. She's said nothing about it, and I wouldn't expect it. They're curious why I spend so much time there, too."

"Ah, here he is." Kirk reached for the mouse, but before he could click to call Wally, Wally called him, so he clicked "answer" instead.

"Good evening, folks." Wally was using his usual dim lighting, so they could mostly only see the outline of his bald head and large, pointed ears. "Sorry I'm late. Is Ruby there yet?"

Marissa moved her chair closer to the screen. "She can't make it. She's off on a rescue mission."

"Then let's begin." Wally reached forward to type, his bulging eyes reflecting his screen. "What's this, a new song?"

"That's for later," Kirk said. "I thought we'd start by adding your tracks to the new version of 'Oops.' I took your suggestion about cutting a lot of words. Sent you a recording."

"I see it. Let's have a listen." Wally reached for his headset, which smushed his ears flat when he put it on. He nodded his head while listening, and took notes offscreen.

"Ruby is getting better," Wally said at the end. "Let's see what I can do with this." He rolled his chair back, grabbing his electric guitar as he stood beside the mic. He was a weird dark silhouette against the white wall, hunched over the guitar with his translucent membranes hanging like a short veiny cape.

At the end of the session, Kirk helped Marissa return her drum kit to the spare office. "That went well, I thought. We're really lucky to have him. He'll be amazing on the album."

The album. Marissa bit her lip. Despite having agreed to it, she worried. It would be great to work on a big project like that with Kirk, and the songs were pretty good, but were they really ready? Like, *really* really? Like, rent a real studio ready? Ruby had literally been playing for just weeks, and while Marissa had been drumming on things since she was a child, only in the last year had she begun to annoy her family with actual drums. When Kirk had raised the idea during their last session, Wally had just said, "Hm." He probably thought it was a bad idea but was just too polite to say so. On the other hand, when had he ever been polite?

Kirk slipped the computer into its bag and looked around for anything else. "Can I drop you somewhere?"

The sensible thing would be to hop on a subway and get home, to avoid a conversation about where have you been you said you'd be back by six. That also felt like the least scary thing. But being sensible and safe had its limits. She took a deep breath. "I have a little time, if you'd like to grab a coffee." Not having planned this, she wasn't ready with a reason, so she stopped there, kicking herself for not having figured out some pretext, feeling like a fool.

But Kirk just shrugged. "Sure. Got everything? Then let's go."

Five

Ruby rose early as usual. She tapped on the door of Charlie's room and waited until there was movement within. It was about a forty-five minutes' walk to Danno's, but when she'd lived here before, nobody had objected to her use of George's old bicycle, and anyway she had no intention of asking permission. A little breakfast, a few sandwiches to take along for lunch, and they could be on their way.

As she took out a skillet and ingredients, she looked at the wall clock. Six a.m. That was sixteen hours since Speck had vanished. Even if he came straight here, even at top speed, even if he could go that fast for hours on end, even if he could tell which way she was from that distance, it was too early to expect him. She put it out of her mind and focused on sandwich-making.

Charlie came down yawning, still in pajamas. Ruby, standing at the stove stirring scrambled eggs, looked him over critically. "We need to get going soon."

"I just need a minute." He came over to look into the skillet. "There's white in those eggs."

"Why, yes, there is. Your point?"

"I don't like the whites. I like them mixed up more."

Him and Simon. "You understand if I did that, the whites would still be in there, right?"

"But I wouldn't see them. They're gross."

"Eat with your eyes closed, then. I'm not cooking another batch."

"I'll just have toast."

Men. Everything would be so much simpler without them. "Suit yourself, but hurry. We're out of here in fifteen minutes. Do you have a bike?"

"Yeah."

Even this early, she could feel the weather would be oppressive—hot and muggy. Danno's house was southeast of town, on a road that wound between a bunch of little lakes. It was a small place, but tidy, because Danno was handy and couldn't stand to see things looking run-down. While there were some things he wasn't great at, he could look after himself if he just had someone to take care of the financial end of things. Not his mom, unfortunately.

Charlie pulled up beside her in the driveway of Danno's house—she'd ridden only just slow enough for him to stay in sight. "I thought we were going to the woods."

"First I want to see if anyone's at home." Ruby put the kickstand down and went over to stand on tiptoe and look through the window in the garage door. There was a car in there. Danno didn't drive, but Ruby had forgotten to ask whether his mom had taken the car when she went.

Charlie was standing at the front door, waiting.

"Did you ring the bell?"

"Yeah. Wasn't I supposed to?"

Ruby stopped at the living room window. "Better ring again."

Charlie pressed the button several times. The bell was audible, but there was no sign of life.

"All right." Ruby headed for the bikes. "Off we go."

"Hang on. I hear swearing."

Ruby turned back. In a minute, the door opened, and Annie Far-rugia looked out at them, leaning against the door frame. She was a mess, hair tangled and makeup smeared. "What do you want? Do you know what time it is?"

"Is Danno home?"

"How would I know? I just got back myself."

Ruby restrained the urge to slap her. "Where have you been? Did you actually talk with anyone since you got back? They put him in emergency foster care."

"Why the hell would they do that? He's a big boy."

"He's a minor, Annie. He ran away from the foster family. Can you just check if he's here?"

Annie turned without a word and walked back into the house, leaving the door open. After a minute, she returned. "He'll turn up."

Ruby leaned in, looking up at her from inches away. "They'll take him away from you. Do you understand? You can't just run off and leave him alone. If it was the sheriff here instead of me, you'd probably be under arrest."

"Well, f—" Annie glanced at Charlie. "Fudge. We'll get out of town, then." She waved at the house. "This is a rental. What do I care?"

What did this woman even do for money? Ruby decided not to ask or speculate. "I came out here to try and find him."

"Fine, I'll pack a few things, and you call me when you find him. Thanks for the warning about the sheriff. I won't answer the door."

Charlie looked back over his shoulder as they walked back to the bikes. "That's pretty messed up."

"You're not kidding." Ruby slung a leg over the bike. "Let's go."

It was just another minute to the path leading into the woods. Ruby laid the bikes out of sight behind some bushes and shouldered her backpack. "Any particular place you've seen the... leaf people before?"

"No, I think they're just around." Charlie walked beside her, looking around the thick woods. "I haven't seen them close to the path, though."

Ruby pulled up a map on her phone. The path wasn't shown, but they were heading more or less for the center of the wooded patch. They walked on a few minutes, looking and listening.

The oak trees cast a dense shade in the heart of the wood, and there was less undergrowth. "Okay." Ruby stopped and marked their location on the map so they could find it again. "Let's get away from the main path." They went down a deer trail, single file, then alongside a gully, until Ruby judged they were far enough off the beaten path. She sat on a large fallen log, patting the place she wanted Charlie to sit.

Charlie boosted himself up. "Do you think they'll come?"

"If they're around, I expect they've noticed us." She unzipped her backpack and took out a piece of cardboard to which she'd taped a printout of the Goodnight Agency logo, a long crescent with two little crossbars.

"What's that for?"

Ruby leaned the sign against the log. "This is the… the international symbol for people who help fairies."

"How do you know that?"

"I can't tell you."

"What if *they* don't know about it?"

"That's why I brought you along. If they see me with you, they might think I'm okay, too."

Charlie looked around. "You think they're watching us now?"

"Well, they don't have TV, and there's just not that much interesting stuff going on in the woods, so yeah, I think they might be watching and listening to hear me say they should tell Danno that Ruby and Charlie are here looking for him."

"They don't talk."

"I hope they can listen, though. They should tell him his mom is back. He doesn't need to hide out anymore." She took her book out of her backpack. "We can wait here while they get him. Want to learn more about freaky Cambrian critters?"

"I think you should call them *creepy* Cambrian critters." He shifted closer to see the pages.

About twenty minutes later, Ruby's phone pinged with a text from Marissa. *Can we talk?*

Not right now, Ruby answered. *On fairy patrol can text*

I sort of went on a date with Kirk

Sort of?

Just coffee but he just talked about robots the whole time

Ruby looked around. Charlie was still absorbed in the book, and no fairies were in sight. She didn't know how to answer. That's just what a get-together with Kirk was like—he talked about robots or rockets or a game or music or a book, and you talked about it, too. Maybe Marissa had hoped for something else, but romance was not Ruby's thing, and she wasn't sure what that would be. Was he supposed to lean across the lattes and tell her she had pretty eyes? It all seemed kind of silly. Still, M was awaiting a reply, so she should come up with something.

That's too bad

IKR what am I supposed to do with that

Charlie squeezed her arm. She looked up and followed his gaze to a dark tree-trunk behind a bay bush. What was he looking at? Then she saw it, starting with the eyes. A creature about her height, face dark and creased as oak bark, over a garment of leaf and vine, blending in so well with the shadowed forest that it might have been standing there all along. Slowly, so as not to startle it, quickly texted, *L8r,* switched the phone to silent, and set it aside

. Heart hammering, she forced herself to be still, looking in its direction without staring right into its dark green eyes. Oh! There was another one, seated on the leaf litter. And another standing behind it.

"Thank you for helping Danno," she said softly. "He'll be safe with us. Then nobody else will come through your home looking for him."

The seated one glanced up at the one near the tree. That one looked at her, challenging. She touched her sign. "Simon sent me. You knew him years ago. He's grown up now and helps people like you."

Oak considered this for a few seconds, then nodded to Leaf-litter. It scrambled to its feet and away, making no sound with its big bare feet. They waited.

Even knowing where they were, they were hard to see. Ruby looked around for more, trying to unfocus and take in shapes. "Is there anything you need?"

Oak shrugged.

Charlie piped up. "How many of you live here?"

The remaining two consulted silently, then Oak raised both hands, four long twiggy fingers on one hand, two on another.

Only six. Her heart sank. Simon had said there were nine. How much longer could they survive here? "Simon can arrange to move you, if you like. There are wilder places, farther from towns. Maybe there are others like you." How would that work? She could hardly imagine them piling into a bus and rolling along the interstate, but apparently there were ways.

Oak's eyes widened, and it clutched at the tree trunk as if someone were trying to tear it away. The other one shifted from foot to foot.

"I get it. This is home. It's up to you, if you ever need it. I'm just afraid someone will…" The creature looked so distraught Ruby stopped, unwilling to distress it further with talk of developers and chainsaws. "…cause you trouble here." Again moving slowly, she reached into her bag for a sphere of black glass. "I'll leave this here. If you break it, we'll come." She set it on the log.

"All right, I'm coming! Wait up!" The voice was distant. Ruby half-stood to turn and look, and the two fairies vanished in an instant.

"Over here!" she shouted. "Danno, it's Ruby!"

"Okay, hang on, I'm stuck!"

Ruby grabbed Charlie's hand, and they made their way in his direction as fast as they could. They found him just getting loose from a blackberry bush, and he gave them a huge grin. "Hey guys. What are you doing here?"

Charlie ran up and gave him a hug. "We came looking for you. Everyone's worried about you."

That wasn't strictly true—his mother hadn't seemed especially concerned. But it was close enough that Ruby didn't feel it necessary to offer a correction. "Your mom's home. You need to get out of here."

Danno thumped Charlie's back, looking regretful. "I was okay, honest. I, uh, someone helped me." He looked at the ground.

"Yeah, we know about them. It's okay. But it's a problem for them that you're here, so you have to come away."

"They'll send me back to those people."

The foster family, he probably meant. They would if they caught him. It was a difficult situation, but he clearly couldn't stay here. He looked thinner than she remembered, and he'd already been thin. His clothes were filthy. He hadn't washed in a long time and had shadows under his eyes. Even with fairy help, he could only manage so long. "Come on, I've brought sandwiches and water."

His eyes brightened. "I could have a sandwich."

He would've had *all* the sandwiches, but Ruby stopped him after two, concerned that too much on what was clearly an empty stomach would be bad for him. He sipped at a Coke bottle of lukewarm water as they walked. Ruby pulled up the map again, but the GPS showed her downtown, which was obviously incorrect. She held it up to the sky. Her position jumped to the middle of a nearby lake.

"It's that way," Charlie said. "I just saw one waving at us."

Whatever. Ruby put her phone away and let him take the lead. Soon enough they were back on what she assumed was the path they'd come in on. When car noises told her they were close to the main road, she turned to Danno. "The police are looking for you, so you should wait here, okay? We'll have your mom come and get you."

Danno looked mournful. "We're gonna run away again?"

Ruby sighed. She was beginning to see that finding Danno had been the easy part. Untangling his situation was going to be a lot trickier. How many times had they run? Enough for him to recognize the pattern. Was Annie running from something more than just her responsibilities? Either way, it was a losing proposition. The sheriff must have a warrant with Annie's name on it, and if she was stopped by any officer for anything, it would show up on their computer. Maybe even in other states. Didn't they all share information? If she just delivered Danno back to his mom, he wouldn't be any better off than he was now. He'd just end up in foster care again, only this time his mom would be in jail.

Charlie must've seen it on her face. "What are you thinking?"

"I'm thinking I'm about to get into trouble again." Ruby reached for her phone. And it was off.

"**What did you** mean, going off like that without a word?" Alfonso Gomez loomed over his daughter, scowling.

"Since when do I have to specifically tell you where I'm going?" Marissa scowled back, crossing her arms. "That's why I share my calendar with you."

"Right after you were in a house where there was an attempted murder. This is not a normal time! Niña, you should have better sense!" He paced in front of her. "You used to be such a good girl. Now since you met those *malhechores*, you just get worse and worse." He gestured at her head, and she shrank back a little. "The hair, the ugly clothes. Don't you want to be a girl anymore? You used to look so pretty, and now it's like a butcher cuts your hair! We moved to a good neighborhood, a safe neighborhood, not so you could go to murder-houses and be questioned by police!"

"You were happy enough to have me go there when she was offering to pay my tuition! And come on, that house cost like fourteen million dollars. It's hardly a gang hangout. That sort of thing can happen to anyone."

He waggled a finger in her face. "All of a sudden it happens a lot to people you know! That girl's uncle, he was arrested for murder—"

"And cleared!"

"Also his friend was murdered—"

"You can't count that twice. It's the same murder."

"If you interrupt me again, it will not be so well for you." Her dad's accent always got stronger when he was upset. "This Olga person you brought into that house, how do you even know her? The detective says she's in a gang."

A pause. "Well?" he said.

"Sorry, didn't want to interrupt you. I met her through Ruby."

"That girl again!"

"Olga quit the gang. She wants to get away from that stuff. She's an artist."

"And yet, the very day she goes there, a murder!"

"Stop. It wasn't a murder. And you know as well as I do Olga has no reason to hurt Ms. Wheelwright."

He snorted skeptically. "And then there were those questions about the old building that so mysteriously fell down."

"You know that I was right here watching TV with you when that happened."

He swooped his arm around. "Not the point. You meet this Ruby person, and three times in two months, the police, they want to talk with you. You turn into"—He gestured to her whole person—"this. You sneak out. You talk back. And I have seen these videos you made. That is not decent music for a good Catholic girl."

"Oh, my God, are we back in the fifties? It's just rock, Daddy."

"What happened to your nice friends from school?"

"Dad, they were never nice. Ashley is mean. All of them are fake.

All they care about is appearance and gossip. My new friends accept me for who I really am."

"Feh." He pointed. "*This* is who you really are? Next you tell me you want to ride motorcycles and date women."

Motorcycles were ridiculously dangerous, and she had no interest in dating women. "If I did, that would be my business. There's nothing wrong with that!"

"These people have corrupted you. You are not to see them anymore or go to that woman's house."

"That's not fair! Until when?"

"What do you mean, until when? Until I die. Then you can do what you like, when I'm not there to see."

"You can't tell me who I can be friends with!"

"I think you will find that I can." He turned to leave her room.

"In that case, I quit soccer!"

He paused, then looked back over his shoulder. "Suit yourself. Since you have free time now, I'll ask Father Hernandez if he knows some better activities you can join. Maybe choir."

"O-o-o-oh!" She slammed the door after him and flumped onto her bed. She looked at her phone and saw there was a new text from Ruby, unnoticed during the recent... discussion. *It was just (angel emoji)(devil emoji).* What was that supposed to mean? *Where u?* she texted back.

(airplane)

What the hell? Thought u left yesterday

Mission accomplished coming home. (coffee) 2nite tell all

Marissa sighed. *Can't grounded 4 life*

(eyeroll) Again? Why? NM it's no devices time l8r

Damn.

There was a scratching at her door, and she opened it to let in McSchmidt, their German Shepherd/Scottie mix. He wasn't allowed on the furniture—she patted the bed, and he jumped up, tail wagging.

She sat and ruffled his ears. "Who does he think he is, telling me who I can see?"

McSchmidt had no answer but put a paw on her leg and gave her a consolatory lick on the chin.

"You're right, he doesn't get to. In fact, I'll call Olga right now."

The dog offered no objection, so she dialed Ms. W's house.

William picked up. *"Wheelwright residence."*

"William, hey. It's Marissa. How is she?"

"Still unconscious, I'm told. Mister Underwood is with her at the hospital now."

Mr. Underwood would be the nephew, Terrence. "Do they still think someone poisoned her?"

"They haven't said, but the police are still investigating, so one presumes they believe so."

Right, one does. "How are you doing, William?"

"It's a fraught time, Miss Gomez."

William describing something as "fraught" was like a normal person running in circles screaming. "You must be so worried about her."

"We are all very concerned, of course. Will you be coming over?"

"Can't, I'm afraid, but is Olga there?"

"I believe Miss Gregoiovich is in the kitchen. Do you wish to speak with her?"

"Please."

"Remember to observe the niceties." The phone switched to hold music.

Observe the niceties was the household code for, *assume you can be overheard.* Did William really think the police were tapping the phone line? Maybe so—Ms. W was a big wheel in the mundane world as well as in the Scene, and the house was packed to the gills with suspects.

"Yah?"

Marissa shifted the phone to her other ear, freeing up a hand to rub the dog's chest. "Yah yourself. I wasn't sure you'd still be there."

"*Thought they'd haul me off in irons? They still might. Or Terrence could fire me, I guess. He seems to be in charge here for now.*"

"I hope he doesn't, but what I meant was I wasn't sure you'd want to stay after this. I feel bad that I brought you into this mess."

"*Oh, foo. It's an adventure, and hey, a job is a job. Good thing the cook is still missing, though, or I'd be in the spotlight.*"

Observe the niceties. "Do they… have any leads on that?"

"*Margo came up with a photo, so probably they're scouring the streets.*"

Not, presumably, a real photo of the Goloopa. There were other questions she wanted to ask, but it seemed she would need to be there to ask them. "Will you let me know if there's any way I can help? You or anyone there?"

"*I'll pass the word, but it's mostly just waiting right now.*"

Waiting to learn whether Ms. W would make it, to find out what the police would come up with. Marissa put her phone on the charger and rolled to the other side of the bed to look out her window, three floors down to the street. The hip grocery across the way was busy with late afternoon shoppers.

What could she do, anyway?

She'd told Ruby she was grounded, but actually she hadn't been told to stay home—just to avoid certain people. But those were exactly the people she needed to see to help resolve matters.

But there was another way to influence things, from home. Maybe she could use the special ability Ms. W seemed convinced she possessed. Could she fix things by tweaking?

Those matters involved herself, though, which complicated things. Ruby had seemed skeptical, but it really was true that she saw most clearly how to affect things that didn't touch on herself directly. Anything about herself was fuzzed out in the vision, and Ms. W was pretty close, so she should expect the ability to be even less reliable than usual where she was concerned. But if she chose her goals carefully, maybe she could get things back on track indirectly.

She stretched to the nightstand for the pen and paper she used to write down night thoughts. So—goals for her vision.

Number one, make Ms. W wake up and be okay. There probably wasn't anything she could do to affect that, but it was worth a try.

Number two was an easy call—bring the attempted killer to justice.

Number three… she wanted to say make her parents be reasonable about her seeing her friends and going to Ms. W's, but that involved her directly. How about, make the album happen? No, that might just mean they would make it without her. Number three—let Ms. W have her protégé again. There, that didn't actually mention her, but it should get her back in the door at Ms. W's. And if her parents allowed that, they'd probably be okay with Ruby and Kirk, too. Probably.

She gave McSchmidt a final scritch and pat, sat up cross-legged on the bed, and went into her trance, keeping her goals in mind. The noises from the street were a distraction, and McSchmidt pushed his cold nose into her curled hand, but she cleared away outside sensations one by one, and eventually the vision came to her, looking up from beneath at the symbols that represented everything going on around her. She was used to seeing Ms. W in there as a huge node like a spider at the center of a web, only instead of a spider, she was represented by a china teacup. The teacup was still there but less prominent. Only a few threads and struts now led to it. Did that mean she wasn't going to get better? That her influence had ended? Other objects in her field of view represented other people—some she didn't know, or at least maybe she knew them but didn't recognize their symbols—like, who was the little race car? What was this, anyway, a game of Monopoly? Other nodes represented abstractions, and among others, she recognized the one for the ability to nudge future events, still tenuously attached to Ms. W.

Keeping her three goals in mind, she began to experimentally push and tug on anything movable, trying to see what might make things fall into the desired configuration, and what was the nudge she'd have to do to make that happen.

Assuming all this wasn't simply her imagination.

The door swung partway open, and that Spider character stuck his head into the kitchen. "Coast clear?"

Olga looked up from her pot of sofrito, shoving hair from her face with the back of her hand. "Clear of what?"

"Cops."

"At the moment, but they could pop up anytime." She checked the two timers on the counter. Where the hell had Margo gone? It's not that she was much use in the kitchen, but it was still better than cooking everyone's meals by herself. She was starting to understand why the Goloopa was always so cross.

Spider came the rest of the way into the room and aimed for the fruit bowl. "Folks still in hiding, then. Do you want a hand in here?"

"Sure. Can you roast those peppers over the stove?"

"Pepper roasting is my specialty." He rummaged through a pottery canister of cooking utensils and pulled out a long two-pronged fork.

Olga kept an eye on him to make sure he really knew what he was doing. Two days after the unfortunate dinner party, he was the only guest still in the house. Had Ms. W intended to put him up? Terrence apparently either didn't mind or was too busy to care.

Spider saw her watching, grinned, and held up a blackened pepper. "How many are we cooking for?"

"Just five, um, humans." Weird way to talk, but she'd already been told three times that "they're all people." She peeked into the oven. "The others must have some food stashed wherever they're hiding."

He looked around at the various bowls and pans. "Are you over-doing it a bit?"

"I want there to be leftovers. Also, I don't know how safe my job is with Terrence in charge, so I want to make a splash."

He speared a new pepper. "Do you think he'll still honor the tuition thing?"

"You know about that?" Apparently it was the regular deal. "I don't know, but even if he doesn't, it's a decent job with lodging, so I don't have to go back home."

He raised an eyebrow. "Have to?"

She flushed. Something about this man made her talk too much. "What's your business with Ms. W?"

"None. I just stay here sometimes when I roll into town. Reckon I'll head out early tomorrow if I get the go-ahead. So tell me, who do you think did it?"

It was a thing nobody was talking about, at least not to her, and she'd wondered whether they were all looking at the new girl, the Southsider, as the main suspect, and talking among themselves about her. "I don't know what reason anyone would've had."

He rotated the pepper, angling the fork carefully to prevent it slipping off. "If it's money, I'm guessing Terrence stands to inherit. I don't know of other relatives. But there might be something in the will for William and Margo, too. Still, I think it's more likely Doctor Sin."

"Because…?"

"Classic love triangle. He's obsessed with her, but she only has eyes for William, who, of course, has no idea. If Sin can't have her, no one can."

"Now you're just making shit up."

"No, think about it. Imagine you had a butler whose last name was Fitzmorgan. Can you honestly tell me you would call him by his first name? 'Get the door, Fitzmorgan. Fitzmorgan, fetch my tea.' Who could resist that? And yet she only uses his first name. There has to be a reason."

She peeked under the lid of the steamer. "They're both, like, eighty years old."

"True love knows no season. You want to roast all of these?"

"Just four. Then check the beans. You read too many murder mysteries." There was a *ding,* and Olga looked up to see which light was flashing. Front door. She looked around at the pots and timers and decided she could leave for two minutes to get the door.

The monitor at the front door showed that detective at the gate, Derek or Eric or whatever. She checked the approved list posted by the console—he was cool to let in. She thumbed the intercom. "Come to the kitchen, okay?" She mashed the open button, waited to see it close behind him with nobody else sneaking through, then hurried back.

When the detective entered, Spider gave a reserved nod. "Derek, glad you're here, man. I need to ask you something."

"If it's about the investigation, they're not telling me a thing."

"Not exactly. I just need to go out of town a few days. Not a problem, right?"

"Maybe a problem, but from what I know, Bill isn't likely to put out an all-points on you when he's got so many better suspects. Where are you planning to go?"

"Secret."

Derek shrugged. "If you ask Bill, he might say no. But it's not like you're a prisoner."

"So, don't ask is what you're saying."

"Much easier all around. Now I have a question for you."

"Shoot."

"Can I interview the rest of the staff? It might speed things along."

They both looked at Olga. Why did they think it was up to her? Sure, okay, she was the one employee present, but it was literally her third day. Whatever. "We're still on lockdown because there are a couple of officers here to watch over Ms. Wheelwright, but wait in the conservatory, and I'll see what I can do."

"You told them to do *what?*"

Ruby looked carefully at Simon, who this time had *actually* plunged his hands into his hair, making it stick up. She was pretty sure he'd heard her the first time. "I told Danno's mom to bring him here. If I'd just let them take off, who knows what might've happened to them, and I'd never know."

"Why am I only finding out about this now?"

"Because you don't return my calls. Then I was going to tell you when you picked me up at the airport, but you sent Alice instead, so…."

Simon opened his mouth, then shut it. "Fair enough. But why here? What do you expect me to do with them? Does this look to you like a halfway house?"

"Um, kind of, yeah. If there was a qwilliq or something in trouble, you'd put it up here. I don't see why you wouldn't do the same for a couple of humans."

This seemed to give him pause. He smoothed his hair and paced in front of his desk. "That's not the business I'm in. I might eventually get paid for housing qwilliqen."

Ruby relaxed a little. From past arguments, she knew if she could get him talking instead of just saying no, she could generally get to yes. And she'd had time on the plane to think about her strategy. "And you might *not* ever get paid, too. We do some free stuff, right?"

"Yes, we have *pro bono* cases, but humans have other options when they're in trouble. The people we help have only us. If I fill up the spare room with this pair, I might have to turn away a legitimate client. Plus, how would they get along with any clients who come here? Would they freak out? Can they keep secrets?"

She raised three fingers. "First, they won't both be staying here, just Danno. He already is friends with fairies and so on, so I think he'll be fine. *She's* going to rehab. That's part of the deal." Lowered a finger. "Second, it's not like you get nothing out of it. Danno is very handy.

Weren't you just telling me you're so busy you have no time to fix things around the house? He can do that, plus he can garden. I noticed the basil is starting to bolt." Last finger. "Third, the attic apartment has two beds if you count the foldout, so however you arrange us, you still have room for a client."

Simon leaned against his desk and drummed his fingers on its edge. "We can't have you and him together in the attic apartment."

"Sure you could. He's not at all dangerous—his brain just works a little different."

"Differently."

"Whatever. Anyway I can defend myself." She dropped into eppy.

"Very amusing." Simon looked past her, possibly thinking of the long list of things that needed fixing, cleaning, and painting. "How long would he be here?"

"Rehab doesn't have a set length. Thirty or sixty days, generally. I looked it up."

"Who pays for this treatment?"

"Danno's mom has some money at the moment. I was careful to not ask where she got it."

Simon sighed. "Fine, we can give it a try."

"Yes!"

"If either of them cause a problem, he goes to foster care. When are they arriving?"

"If they drove straight through like they said they were going to, allowing for lunch and gas stops, any minute now. I thought they could have dinner here."

"Oh, you thought that, did you?"

"I got extra of everything at the deli."

"I'll need her to sign some papers, in case the authorities find him here."

"I thought you might say that, so I called Stefon and explained the situation. If you look on the printer, I think those are the papers you'll need. I also emailed you my notes of what he said. Technically, Minnesota might say she's guilty of kidnapping her own son, which sounds pretty ridiculous to me. But they're unlikely to prosecute that if she gets herself cleaned up, and you should be in the clear either way if you have the right paperwork."

Simon's expression wavered between annoyance and amusement. He stood, straightening his face and his jacket. "Let me know when they arrive."

"There's one other thing I wanted to talk about."

"I have things to do, and so do you, unless you've had more time to prepare for Saturday than I think. Can you make it brief?"

"Don't worry about that, I'll be ready for the Skohlars. It's about Cousin Charlie."

Simon went around behind his desk and pulled out the chair. "Meg's youngest? What about him?"

"They're sending him to a boarding school that sounds absolutely horrific. Can't you talk to Aunt Meg about it?"

"I *have* talked to her. It's shameful, I agree. I'd hoped I could get them to at least choose a school that wasn't abusive, but Ralph thinks he needs 'toughening up,' apparently. You know what he's like—I don't think sticking my oar in again will get any better results. I'm open to ideas about how to improve matters, so long as it doesn't involve bringing Charlie to live here as well. We're collecting quite enough of your rescue projects for the moment." Simon sat. "If there's nothing else?"

Ruby took her backpack out into the small courtyard in back. This yard had paths winding among flower beds and a small gazebo, which had become her favorite reading spot. She grabbed a cushion off a wicker armchair, put it on the railing near a corner, and sat, propping her feet on the opposite railing and leaning back against the cool, rough stone of the courtyard wall. Just in case, she checked the tube on the backpack strap, but Speck wasn't in it. If he'd really gone racing to Minnesota after her and was now headed back, he must still have a long way to return. But she had hoped he'd just come home and wait for her.

Oh, well. She took out her computer, opened the file of Skohlar material, and began to read.

Six

Olga had a few minutes before the Big House Meeting, so she fired up her computer to check her email. It was a battered reconditioned laptop, the screen held on with an improvised hinge her brother had screwed into the plastic. With any luck, it would last until she saved enough for a better one.

There was a new email from Marissa.

I know you like art, but I'm not sure if you do any sculpture or pottery. If you're interested, there's a little clay studio with a wheel, kiln, and other tools in the basement. My folks aren't letting me go over there at the moment, but Kate can set you up if you like.

She did like. Drawing was her usual thing, but in this house full of art, some of the pieces made her think of things she'd like to try, experiments with shape.

Thanks, she wrote back. *I'll try it.*

There was also an email from her other brother, the one who always had money so was probably doing something illegal, to let her know Deandre had been by looking for her because "I need her to do a thing." Well, let him look. She was done doing things for Deandre and not planning to ever again be where he could find her.

She checked her watch and hurriedly shut the computer down, running downstairs to the drawing room where the others were already gathered.

Sitting in a circle near the front windows were Terrence, William, Margo, the detective Derek, and that lady cop, Urbana. That was all the humans in the house, then, since Spider had left bright and early. What was this about? Hopefully she wasn't the subject of this meeting. She sat on the window seat, sunshine warming her back.

Terrence looked up from his phone and cleared his throat. "We're all here. Good. I wanted to give y-you all an update on Priscilla's condition and, um, pool our knowledge of the state of the investigation."

Olga let go the breath she'd been holding. It was not about her. With the old lady out of the picture for now, she'd been sure Terrence was going to kick her out.

Terrence waggled his phone. "I have the doctor's report here. I'm Priscilla's designated medical whatchacallit, so they have to tell me. She had a"—he consulted the screen—"ischemic stroke brought on by an overdose of methamphetamine." He looked around at the group. "I hope I don't need to tell you that she doesn't use drugs or in fact take anything stronger than an occasional small glass of sherry. So, it wouldn't take a lot of meth for her to overdose. They tell me it's uncertain whether she'll recover or to what extent."

Derek looked at Urbana. "Do you know whether it was in the soup?"

"I haven't been allowed to see the case files, and I haven't wanted to press since it's not my department. Given what you all have told me about the night's events, though, that seems a reasonable assumption."

Terrence tucked his phone away. "Of course we all, uh, want the kill—I guess I can't say killer—the attacker brought to justice." He smoothed the nonexistent hairs on top of his head. "Nearly as urgently, we want the police visits to stop so we can take the house off lockdown. If this goes on much longer, we'll have to sneak all the nonhumans out and find somewhere else for them to stay, not an easy matter."

Urbana crossed her arms. "In hopes of speeding that along, I don't suppose anyone present would like to confess? If it was one of you, I'll find you anyway, and it won't be pleasant for you."

Terrence laughed nervously but waited along with everyone else. No one was particularly looking at Olga, which was reassuring.

"Very well." Urbana sat up and put her hands on her lap. "What do we know about motives? Terrence, I expect you're the main beneficiary of Priscilla's will?"

"We won't see it unless she, uh, passes, but I expect so, yes. I don't know for sure if anyone else here stands to inherit, but I'd be surprised if there weren't something for the longtime staff." He gestured at Margo and William.

"We have decent pension plans," Margo said. "We get that regardless. She never discussed her will with me." She looked at William, who shook his head.

"But you make her appointments," Urbana said. "Has she met with the lawyer who handles her will since she met Marissa Gomez? Or even looked at her copy?"

Margo looked thoughtful. "You mean, might she have changed her will in favor of Marissa? I don't know. She meets with that lawyer often, and I don't always know why."

What were they *saying?* "Hey!"

They all looked at Olga.

"You can't seriously think Marissa poisoned her."

"We're just considering motive here," Derek said. "This is what the detectives on the case are doing. Of course, they don't know about Marissa being 'The One,' so if they got a copy of the will and she's mentioned, they'll wonder why. They'll wonder *really hard.*"

"If she's in there," Olga said, "I'm sure she doesn't know."

"Even if Ms. Wheelwright has just been talking about changing her will," Derek said, "that could be motive for a current heir who might be cut out."

Terrence looked uncomfortable. "I don't think she talked to anyone about her will, ever."

Urbana leaned forward. "So who else do you *think* might stand to inherit?"

Terrence shrugged. "I, uh, expect there'd be a big chunk for some charities. Doctor Sin is on the board of a couple of her favorite ones, but they're not *that* desperate for cash."

Urbana made a note in her notebook, nonetheless. "Any other reason you know of, or anyone else who might have a grudge?"

Olga decided not to mention Spider's far-fetched love triangle theory. No one else spoke.

"Come on," Urbana said. "It wasn't an accident, so *someone* did it. If you don't want to speak in front of this group, we can talk in private, but one of you must know something that can help."

After a minute of uncomfortable silence, Margo raised her hand. "You only talked about why. What about how it was done? Who had access to her bowl?"

Olga tensed. That was a question that put the spotlight right on her. "I took the tray straight from the kitchen. The Goloopa told me to serve Ms. W last, so I guess I carried her bowl to every place at the table."

"Wait." Urbana opened her notebook. "You were specifically told to serve her last? Was that usual?"

Olga had to shrug, but Terrence answered. "She likes to see guests served first. More hospitable."

"So that wasn't just the Goloopa trying to spread the suspicion around." Still, she made a note. "So you were, what, holding the tray in one hand and reaching between people to set bowls down with the other hand?"

"Pretty much."

"So someone might've twisted around to put something into a bowl while you were busy setting one down?"

Olga stood and positioned her arms to show how she'd been holding things, leaning over Derek as if to set a bowl in front of him. "They'd have to reach awful far, and I don't see how they could tell which bowl was hers without standing to look down in them. Plus, they might *put* it in, but I don't see how they would *mix* it in."

"Priscilla stirred it herself," Terrence said. "But how could they be sure she would do that?"

"Hm." Urbana made another note. "I don't get the impression this was planned. For one thing, there are far more effective poisons they could've used. So nobody was standing?"

Olga dropped her imaginary tray and sat. "None of the guests, and William was out of the room. I saw the Goloopa fill the bowls in the kitchen. The last few, anyway. They could've put something in, but I don't see how anyone else could've messed with her bowl before it was on the table. Except me, of course, but I didn't. But hang on a minute. Derek is right about the meth—it's not a sure way to kill someone. But an overdose is pretty risky, especially for an old person, so it's not just someone's idea of a joke."

Urbana arched an eyebrow. "Know a lot about meth, do you?"

"Where I grew up you hear a few things. So it's someone who just happened to have some on them? Or anyway didn't have enough time to find something better."

"The dinner was just one day's notice," Terrence said. "I suppose even if you knew you wanted to poison someone, you might not be able to come up with the best poison that quickly."

Derek sat up straighter. "But why the big rush? Why did it have to be at that dinner instead of whoever it was taking their time to come up with something more certain? Was someone trying to stop her doing something? Maybe they didn't mean to kill her, only disrupt the dinner."

"It certainly did that," Urbana said. "Getting back to how, though, who was close enough to reach it once it was set down?" She looked at Margo and Terrence. "Just you two, plus Doctor Sin and Mrs. Polacek. Why were they invited?"

Margo shrugged. "She didn't say. Sin is here often on Foundation business, and Netta Polacek has been to tea a few times, especially since Alasdair's death. The way Priscilla operates, it might've been just to give them those presents. The taser for Netta and whatever Sin got."

"I think it was a lipstick," Terrence said. "He tucked it away pretty quick, so I didn't get a close look."

Derek made a note. "You think all these gifts were because she had one of these visions? There'll be a special use for each?"

"Maybe not all. Maybe just the five who were specifically invited." Margo reached into her collar and pulled out a necklace of glass beads with a pendant of iridescent stone set in loops of silver wire. "I think she gave me this just so I wouldn't feel left out. It's a Lioness Elise piece, and she knows I love that stuff. Terrence and I are always here, and Spider was staying over anyway. But the others, yeah, there's some purpose, but there's no way to know what it could be. The reasons she does these things are unpredictable. If she gave Doctor Sin a lipstick, it might be because he'll have an emergency and need something to leave a message, or he might meet a woman who desperately needs that exact shade, and she'll tell him something he needs to know while she's putting it on, or maybe just seeing it at the right moment will give him an idea. We've found there's no point in guessing."

Derek and Urbana asked a few more detail questions, then Urbana set her business card on the coffee table. "If anyone... remembers anything else, please call either of us anytime." Derek threw his card down also, and the meeting was over.

Olga went to the kitchen to start the next in the never-ending sequence of meals there was nobody else but her to prepare. While she consulted the menu cards and cookbooks, hauled out ingredients, she thought things over. Four people near enough to reach the bowl, plus the Goloopa. Could one of them have panicked when she started giving out presents? Like if they figured she was doing her magic on them all and wanted to stop her? But nobody knew what the presents were about.

Olga grabbed the big knife and started in on a bundle of celery. They might just have to wait for the old bat to wake up and tell them, if she ever did.

Ruby found Simon in his office, hunched over stacks of paper. She stopped in the doorway, and he looked up. "Any sign of your rescue project?"

"Not yet. I'm getting worried about them. You shouldn't sit like that. Ujo is always telling me to keep my back straight."

"Good point." He sat up and rolled his shoulders. "Was there something else?"

She hesitated. It made her squidgy to think of talking to someone about this. Normally she would've called Marissa, but the subject was a little… sensitive between them. Besides, he might actually have some useful advice. "Um, yeah, if you have a minute."

"I could use a break." Simon stood, stretched, and walked over to an armchair, motioning her to the settee.

She sat, clasping her hands in her lap. "So, it's like this." How to put it? "Ujo is having me tutor Kirk in fighting."

"I heard."

"I feel funny about it. Kirk kind of—he says he likes me. Don't you dare tell anyone I said that."

Simon made a zipping motion over his lips. "You don't reciprocate?"

"I like him as a friend. So that makes it awkward. You know, I have to touch him during practice, and I have to tell him 'good' or 'wrong' about his stance. Like, he wants approval and not just about the lessons. It makes me uncomfortable. You know?"

Simon nodded. "You already have a complicated relationship, and then you add the teacher-student relationship on top of that. You worry if you praise him, he may take it as encouragement."

"Right. Plus, there's… someone else who likes him, and here I am spending time alone with him."

"And this other person whose name I won't try to guess, you're afraid they might be jealous if they found out?"

"Let's just say she wasn't thrilled when I told her."

Simon's eyebrows rose. "You told her."

"What, you think that's wrong?"

"On the contrary, I'm proud of you."

He was proud of her. Though perhaps also a little surprised. She swallowed back a lump in her throat and had to pause for a moment. "I just figured it'd be worse if she found out later."

"Exactly. Well, this sounds like a tricky situation. Why did you agree to tutor him?"

She squinted at him. "You think *that's* wrong?"

"No opinion yet. Just trying to understand."

"Okay. Well, a few reasons. I really do need a sparring partner. I think I learn from showing him stuff. I don't feel like I'm doing anything wrong. And we both enjoy it."

He nodded. "Those are decent reasons. What do you want from me on this?"

"I don't know. Advice?"

"Very well." Simon rose and walked over to stand and look out the window. He turned around. "The first thing I'd suggest is, you might use a clicker."

"Which is what?"

"They're used to train animals, but also to train people in physical skills. Instead of saying 'good,' you click when he's got it right. That way it's not praise, just feedback. Takes the emotion out of it so you can just focus on learning the skill."

"Okay… I'll think about that."

Simon sat behind his desk. "If you decide to try it, there's a clicker in the rolling cabinet in the basement. Second drawer."

Why would he have one of those?

"As for this third person," he continued, "is there any reason she can't join your sessions?"

"Have her take the class? Isn't it awfully expensive? I don't think he'd teach her for free."

"I was just thinking of the practice sessions, but maybe we can negotiate Ujo's fee, too. A big part of the expense was to get him to have the class at all. It's not any harder to train three people compared to one."

"If you could ask, that'd be great."

"Will do." He jotted a note, then his head swiveled toward the front of the house. "Do I hear a car horn?"

Ruby headed for the door. "That could be them."

It was them. Annie had pulled up at the curb in her beat-up Honda Civic. She and Danno unloaded paper sacks and boxes tied shut with rope from the back seat and trunk. She looked better than she had the last time Ruby'd seen her.

Danno set a large box on the sidewalk at the base of the steps and gave Ruby a big hug. She thumped his back. "What took you so long?"

Annie dropped a bag beside the box, with a clatter. "I'll tell you what took so long. This frickin'—refused to get in the car."

"Oh, really?" Ruby raised an eyebrow at Danno, who blushed.

"We stopped for dinner, and when we left, he just wouldn't get in. We had to walk across the road to a motel instead of driving through like I wanted."

"What'd you have for dinner?"

"The frick difference does that make?" She set down another bag. "I'm just gonna leave this stuff here, or I'll be late."

Ruby picked up a bag. "Late for what?"

"You said I had to go to rehab. Don't seem necessary, but whatever. If that's part of the deal, fine. So I made an appointment—sooner begin, sooner done."

"I was going to get someone to go with you."

"It ain't my first rodeo, honey. You just stick my stuff somewhere, and I'll be back in a few weeks. I just gotta prove I can stay sober for a while."

Simon was leaning against the wall at the top of the stairs, arms crossed. Danno stopped there, a box in his arms, eyes pointed downward. "Where should I...?" He jiggled the box.

"What'd your mom have for dinner?"

"Um, a burger and three beers, sir."

Simon nodded. "You did exactly right. Put everything in the upstairs hallway for now."

Ruby tried to follow with a bag in each hand, but Simon signaled her to wait while he walked down to the car, pulling an envelope from his pocket.

Annie gave him a suspicious look. "What do you want?"

He held out the envelope. "I'll need you to sign where I put the tape flags."

"What is this shit?" She flipped through the papers.

"The legal papers I need in case his presence here becomes known or in case we don't hear from you again. Temporary guardianship, power of attorney."

She shrugged, took the offered pen, and put the papers on the roof of her car to sign. "This ain't gonna do shit. If they were ready to take him from me, papers signed by me ain't gonna stop 'em."

"No, for that we must rely on secrecy. But the papers *will* help prevent me being jailed as a kidnapper, if worse comes to worst. At least, so my attorney assures me."

Annie returned the papers, kept the pen, slammed her car door, and pulled away from the curb. Simon looked at Ruby. "It doesn't seem to me that she's approaching rehab with quite the right attitude."

"Well, no."

"She certainly seems to know how to work the system. Don't you think you're being played here?"

Ruby adjusted her hold on the bags. "Danno *really* doesn't want to go into foster care, and I don't blame him. It's not a great situation, but if Annie can keep it together for another year and a half, he'll be eighteen. Then they can stay together without the government interfering."

"Don't you think he might be better off without her?"

"Oh, sure, except that he loves her."

"Doesn't he need better care than she can give? He seems… simple?"

"You don't understand. *She* needs *him*. He's not simple, he's, um direct, which is something I like about him. He's good at other things. He'd be *fine* if he lived in a world that was made for him. Like many of our clients, I might add. I don't know why you seem to have problems with him just because he doesn't happen to have tentacles or whatever."

Simon raised an eyebrow. "I'll think about that. All right, get all this stuff off the street and then bring the boy down to the kitchen. Since he's awake and sixteen years old, I expect he's hungry."

As she reached the second floor, her phone pinged with a text. She dodged around Danno on his way down, and set the bags against the railing to check the screen.

Kirk: *Can we meet at RotB? I have something for you.*

She answered, *What? I said no presents.*

You need this for the negotiations.

What the hell? She checked her calendar to see where she could fit it in around lunch and lessons. *2:00?*

CU there.

Danno came up the stairs with an extra-large load. "This is all. Where will I sleep?"

He seemed anxious, and Ruby was tempted to tell him he had

to camp out in the hallway as a joke, but that would be mean. She pointed to the door of her room. "There. I'll be upstairs in the attic. If you need anything, knock on the ceiling." Simon had ruled that Danno didn't have "need to know" about the magic door that switched between the dusty attic full of boxes and the apartment. As far as he was concerned, it was just her room up there. "And if we tell you to hide, like if the police come, the attic is where you should go."

He looked stricken. "The police are coming for me?"

"Probably not, but just in case. They still think you're in Minnesota, I hope. So. Are you hungry?"

Revenge of the Bean was busy, and Ruby had to look around a little to find Kirk, at a corner table, hunched over his computer with headphones on, as usual. She stopped at the counter for a dark roast and wove between the tables. He looked up as she approached and took the headphones off. "Hey, I got a new verse for the latest song."

"That's nice, but I don't have a lot of time. You said you had something to help with the"—she looked around to see whether anyone was listening—"negotiations?"

"Yeah, I had an idea, and I've been talking to Seymour."

"You… know Seymour?"

He pointed to a chair. "Never met him, but he sent me an email a few weeks back. I'm surprised you never introduced us. Anyway, I suggested he should come today, too, since he did most of the work on the program, but he couldn't make it."

Since Seymour was a tentacled sea creature currently living somewhere near the Bahamas, this wasn't surprising. But if Seymour wanted Kirk to know that, he could tell him. Ruby sat. "What program are we talking about?"

"I remembered you needed a special device to talk with"—

he looked around—"the folks you'll be meeting with, so I thought it would be easier if you could use your own phone and hear what everyone was saying at once, instead of just the one holding the mic. You can just talk with them normally."

"How does that work?"

"You just fire it up and listen. I'll show you on mine." He handed her his phone, trailing earbud wires. "You listen to that, and I'll play some ultrasonic sounds on my computer. The phone's mic picks up the sounds and just repeats them, shifted down a couple octaves so you can hear."

Ruby put on the earbuds.

Kirk pressed a few keys on his computer. "I edited an old recording to make it ultrasonic."

A high, squeaky voice started talking, saying it wanted to register a complaint. There followed a fairly silly argument about whether a parrot was dead. "How does that sound?" Kirk asked.

"It's still pretty high-pitched. And I can hear you talking over the earbuds, too."

"You're supposed to hear me. We didn't want the program to block out regular sounds." He moved a slider on the screen. "How about now?"

The voices dropped into a more normal range. *E's bleeding demised!* one of them said. "Better." Ruby listened a little longer. "That's enough." She took the earbuds out. "Works great! I know Seymour's a good programmer, but I'm kind of amazed you put this together so quickly."

"For some reason, he already had a program for something similar."

"Well, this is excellent! Thanks! How do I get it on my phone?"

"I can install it from my computer." He held out a hand. "I'll need you to unlock the phone a couple times."

Ruby unlocked and handed it over, sipping her coffee while she watched Kirk hook it to the computer and do his thing with mouse and keyboard. "I want to hear your new verse, but I still think it's too soon to do an album."

Kirk handed her the phone, which was again asking for her PIN. "It might not matter anyway. Marissa's parents are so freaked about this business with Ms. W, I don't know if they'll let her work on it with us."

"She said she was grounded, but I assume that'll end."

"I don't know. I think it might've been the last straw. They know there's a lot going on they don't understand, and it makes them anxious."

Ruby's cup had somehow emptied itself while she wasn't paying attention. She stood to see whether there was a line at the counter. "Unfortunately, I don't think explaining it to them will do any good. Be right back."

When Ruby returned, Kirk was talking on her phone. "Yeah, here she is." He handed it over.

She covered the mic. "Did you answer my phone?"

"Sorry. It rang while I was holding it, and I panicked."

"Don't do it again." She held the phone to her ear. "Hello?"

"Ruby!" It was Uncle Simon. *"I need you at home immediately."*

"Hang on." She waved the phone at Kirk. "Are you done with what you need to do here?"

"You should be all set."

"Great. Thanks again. Extra super thanks. Sounds like there's an emergency. Gotta go." She grabbed a cup cover on the way to the door and juggled her bag and phone in her other hand. "On my way. What's going on?"

"Have you spoken to Spider recently?"

"Not since that memorable dinner party."

"Any idea where he is?"

She stopped at the bus shelter to look at the schedule. "He said he had a job of some kind but no details. The next bus isn't for ten minutes."

"Take a cab. And text me Marissa's number."

Ruby called a ride-share car—app for emergency use only—and got home seven minutes later. A Hummer with darkened windows was pulled up in front of the house, and that could mean only one thing—Sasquatch. She leaped up the front steps and let herself in, following conversation into the study. Karomeenut, one of the Sasquatch elders, was there in a very nice suit, freshly shaven. This didn't make him look convincingly human, considering the wide black mouth, brow ridge, and protruding ears, but he at least looked prosperous. Dr. Sin was on the settee and Simon in the visitor chair in front of his desk.

"What's up? Has something happened to Spider?"

"Apparently." Simon handed her a sheet of paper.

"He failed to check in yethterday," Karomeenut rumbled. "Thith arrived an hour ago by email."

Ruby looked up, shocked. "But this is a ransom note. Spider's been kidnapped?"

Dr. Sin grimaced. "So someone would have us believe."

"But this doesn't make any sense. Three million?" Ruby shook the sheet at him. "I mean, Spider's a nice guy, but who would pay that kind of money to get him back?"

"Ith not for him." Karomeenut pointed at the sheet with a forefinger the size of a sausage. "Ith for the tho-called cargo. Five of my people."

Five Sasquatches?

"Wild black-maned bigfoots," Simon said. "Recently located and on their way here to join the local community."

The Sasquatch compound was west of the city, disguised as a regular gated community with top-notch security. It was well-forested, but the homes weren't holes in the ground—they were comfortable and modern in style, with huge windows, curved walls, and sod roofs. She handed the sheet back to Simon. "Okay. What can I do?"

"Nothing. Or rather, mind the store here and keep this under wraps while I deal with it."

"Under wraps? From who? Come on, it's not like I was going to call the newspapers."

"Let me clarify." Dr. Sin leaned forward. "No one outside this room is to know of this. The only reason we spoke to you about it, is so you can cover for us."

"So, not Doctor Fortunato? Not even Captain Urbana?"

"*Especially* not her," Simon said. "If she knew, she wouldn't let us pay the ransom. The Guardians have a strict no-negotiation policy. If not, we'd constantly be blackmailed by people threatening to reveal The Scene's secrets."

"But you plan to pay up, anyway?" Three million probably wasn't a huge amount of money to the Sasquatch community, but Captain Urbana might have a point, just this once.

"You mutht underthand. There are fewer than two hundred of uth. Only four other black-maned. We mutht rethcue them."

Dr. Sin raised a finger. "Plus, wild Sasquatch tend not to do well in captivity. We fear they may harm themselves or suffer serious emotional damage if this drags on even a few days. Mister Terboositer's schedule had them making frequent stops to get out of the truck in wooded areas. We need to resolve this quickly."

"And *then* we find theeth people"—the giant finger stabbed at the page—"and dethtroy them. Non-violently, of courthe."

"Of course," Ruby murmured. She'd been told that Sasquatches were gentle, but their size, their claw-like nails, their many scars, and the fact that they had somehow dealt in a final way with one of their own, after Ruby revealed him as a killer, made her wonder how accurate that was. "But who could it be? From the way Spider acted, I thought this was a secret operation. It has to be someone who knew about it, right?"

"That's why I believe Mister Terboositer may have kidnapped himself," Dr. Sin said.

Simon shook his head. "That's really unlikely. I've known Spider for over ten years, and it's just not the sort of thing he'd do."

Dr. Sin scoffed. "For three million dollars, many people might do things they normally wouldn't."

"Reggie, it's not him. Who else knew about this project? Karomeenut, did you talk about this to anyone outside the Sasquatch community?"

"It wath generally known they'd been found. Everyone knew we'd move them eventually. But exactly when and how, only you and Thpider and Ms. Wheelwright."

Simon frowned. "You told *her*? Why?"

"For her to do her thing, make them reach uth thafely."

"That old fraud's blessing does exactly nothing. I hope you didn't give her any money, at least."

Karomeenut shrugged his mighty shoulders. "Chee geth resulth."

"Not this time."

"Whatever." Karomeenut waved a hand. "Get my people back. Worry about finding the mithcreant later."

"Sure." Simon stood. "Fine. We each have things to do, so let's start doing them. Ruby, please let these gentlemen out."

By which he meant, make sure the door locks behind them. Though their old door had been replaced after the police broke it in, the new one had the same problem of not latching unless you pushed it shut. Maybe that was something Danno could look at. Returning from that, she found Simon gone. She went upstairs and stood in his bedroom doorway, watching him take what she thought of as his "action outfit" from the closet. Still a suit but looser fitting, made of shiny material that was easy to clean and, she suspected, cut-proof. "You're going out?"

"I am. Try not to burn the place down while I'm away."

"I've never burned anyplace. Explosions are more my thing."

"None of that either. How is Danno with plumbing?"

"The bathtub leak is already on the list."

"There's something going on with the U-bend in the kitchen, too. If anyone's looking for me, I have the flu."

"Will you be back in time for the Skohlars?"

"Probably not."

"I can't do that alone!"

"You won't be alone. Doctor Sin and Susan will be there, and I think Director Abroft. The Skohlars just want you there—I don't imagine you'll have to say anything. You'll be fine. Excuse me."

Ruby backed out to let him shut the door.

"Which martial art is it, though?" Alfonso Gomez flipped the paper over. Marissa suspected Ruby had created the flyer herself, but it did look reasonably professional.

"It's a variant of Tae Kwon Do. I looked for something that would help me be more coordinated in soccer, and lots of people recommended this."

He looked at her suspiciously. "I thought you were quitting soccer."

"I was just angry. I don't really want to quit."

He handed the flyer back to her. "I won't have to drive you, will I?"

"It's on a bus route."

"All right. What do you need from me, then? A check?"

"I'll ask the first time I go in."

He looked at the clock. "I need to get back to work. Fine. I look forward to your first, what do you call it, where your family can come in and watch?"

That would be tricky, but she'd deal with it when she had to. "Thanks! I'm sure it'll improve my play."

She went back to her room and found a text on her phone from an unrecognized number. It was a photo of a sculpture of a cat, abstract, with flat surfaces and corners. *Who is this?* she texted back.

In a minute the answer came back. *I think supposed to be Sergeant Fuzzbutt. Maybe?*

One of Ms. W's cats, so presumably someone from that house. *No I mean who are you?*

Sorry, this is Margo. Olga has no phone so asked me send pic and say thx for suggestion.

Tell her it's pretty good.

I think so too. Any word about Spider?

What the what? Marissa touched the control to call. "What's this about Spider?" she asked when Margo picked up. "Simon asked me about him, too."

Margo paused. *"Um, observe the niceties."*

"Yeah, yeah, I know. I haven't heard from Spider recently, but it's not like we're best buds or anything. We only just met."

"The, uh, one of Simon's clients hired him for something, and they say he's overdue checking in. No one's said anything to you?"

"No, but I wouldn't worry about him this soon. He didn't strike me as the sort to stick to a schedule."

Silence. What was Margo thinking over there that she couldn't say on an unsecure line? Simon's call had been very brief, just to ask whether she'd heard from Spider in the last day, and Marissa now realized that after her "no," he probably would've liked to ask more, but perhaps he too was cautious of being overheard.

"I might stop by tomorrow," Marissa said at last. She had so many questions about the poisoning, what they'd heard from the police, whether Spider being missing might tie into it, how Olga was doing.

"Maybe we should tell someone in the police he's missing?"

Margo surely wasn't referring to the useless Sergeant Oscher. She must mean the Guardians. "Maybe. But if there's a problem, wouldn't his, um, employer already have done that?"

"I'll have to think about it. See you tomorrow, maybe."

Marissa set her phone aside. Who was this mysterious employer, anyway? She needed someone to talk with about this, but apparently calling them was a bad idea. She opened her door a crack—her dad seemed to have left. The dog, McSchmidt, was still around, though, lounging in her dad's armchair. He slapped his tail against the cushion when he saw her but didn't get up. She rummaged in the fridge and cut some cheddar off the block, then sat on the couch. McSchmidt did stand then to investigate what she was eating, and she broke off a corner for him. "You're an old cheese-hound, aren't you? You're a spaghetti dog."

McSchmidt issued no denials, resting his chin on the chair arm to watch for any other morsels that might come his way.

The police must be looking hardest at the Goloopa, since they were missing, and at Olga since she served the soup, then at the people who were sitting closest. But the detectives on the case didn't know what they were really dealing with. Anyone who'd been associated with The Scene for any amount of time had likely picked up some tricks. Ruby, for instance, probably had already trained Speck to drop something on command wherever Ruby pointed. She could've poisoned the soup. Not that Ruby would do such a thing, of course, but just as an example. Spider had been associating with these people for years— she'd be amazed if he didn't have some tricks up his sleeve.

She broke off another little piece of cheese for McSchmidt. "You aren't allowed on that chair, you know."

Signaling neither agreement nor disagreement, the dog stayed put.

Seven

In the dream, Ruby was in a secret place, a round room where shadows of giants moved across the cloth walls, voices rumbling, just their big feet visible under the edge. She played quietly, not wanting to draw attention, pushing her dump truck toward the edge, around a chair leg and back, until it bumped up against another brown hand like her own. She looked up to a face that looked like hers. The other girl lifted her hand, crane-like, dropping a load of crayons into the truck. Then the wall opened, light flooded in, and large hands reached in for her, setting her down on a roof, alone.

No, not alone. There was Micah again. Ruby walked carefully along the roof peak to where he sat reading a tattered paperback with a picture of a dusty cowboy on the cover. "Simon would call that book trash."

He looked up at her from under his brow ridge. "Simon's a bit of a snob." He set the book aside, keeping a hand on it to prevent it sliding down the slope. "What's the buzz?"

"The usual mayhem. A woman was poisoned, a man was kidnapped, the Skohlars are being fractious, and I have to help get them in line. Oh, and my invisible dog is missing."

"You worried?"

"About which part?" She shrugged. "Being worried is apparently part of the job."

"About the dog, I mean. That's rough."

She sat beside him. "I think he'll be okay. I was on a plane, and he apparently left the plane in flight and got left behind. He doesn't need to eat or drink, so at least he shouldn't starve, but I don't know if he can find his way back. He can track people—that's why I got him. So he should be able to track me, but from how far away?"

Micah put a large hand on her shoulder. "Have faith. I have a feeling he'll be back soon."

"What about you? What are you up to these days?"

"Oh, you know, being dead leaves little time for anything else. That reminds me, though, I have a meeting to get to soon." He looked at his hairy wrist as if expecting to see a watch there.

"Before you go, I want to ask you something. Did you see that other girl again?"

"She's been by. Still can't understand her, but I think her name is Jinju. I mean, she pointed to herself and said that."

"That's my sister. That's Pearl. I just dreamed about her, too, from when we were little."

"I didn't know you had a sister."

"'Had' is the right word. She died."

"I'm sorry."

Ruby shrugged. "I barely remember her—I was like three. She was with my dad when their ferry sank. Hadn't even thought about her for a long time."

"It's funny she looked to be your age, then. I don't seem to have gotten any older since I died." He looked at his wrist again. "Gosh, I'm going to be late. You should go, too." He stood and skated down the slope, book clutched aloft.

"Hey, wait!" Ruby stood, but something slammed into her midriff, and she flailed, opening her eyes to darkness. She felt a thump on her shoulder and tried to push it away, but there was nothing there.

"Stop it!" She sat up, and something whooshed past, tugging at her hair. She groped and turned on the light, fumbling because she wasn't in her usual bedroom, and the switch wasn't in the usual place. The bedside lamp illuminated the low ceiling of the attic bedroom. She was alone.

Then her head jerked back as a shimmer materialized in front of her eyes. "Speck! You're back!" She wanted to hug the little thing, but he wasn't huggable.

Nor did he seem in any mood for affection. He swooped around like an irritated wasp, making little darts at her.

"I'm so sorry I left you behind! I couldn't help it. Hang on, I have a treat for you."

The word "treat" seemed to calm him down. He flew over to her backpack, which sat on a chair below the round front window. She reached in for her "Speck kit"—a flat wooden box containing a few doggie treats, a small metal hoop painted on the inside with blue goop, and an irregular crystal. She ran the crystal around the outside of the hoop, and the opening rippled, looking for a moment like clear water before it settled down to transparency.

She tossed a treat through the hoop, and it transformed, looking like a fluff of thistledown for the second it lasted before Speck swooped upon it. She tossed in another, and it vanished equally quickly.

"That'll do for now." She ran the crystal around the other way to close the ring and put the things away.

On her way downstairs, she noticed Danno's door was ajar, though it was still before six. There was a light on in the first floor hallway, and soft voices coming from the front room. Was Danno awake? Who was he talking to?

She peeked in the door. There was one floor lamp on, and Danno was in the brown armchair, leaning toward someone perched on the ottoman, wearing a… fuzzy green blanket? No one else was supposed to be in the house. No, she saw with a little shock, that was no blanket. The thing on the ottoman was a lanky, green-furred creature, and not only was it not wrapped in a blanket, it appeared to have no clothing aside from sandals. It must've heard her because it turned its head to look, and Danno followed its gaze and smiled at her.

"Um, what's going on?"

Danno pointed. "This is Ekki."

Ekki? Now she recognized the species. It was a wibble—she'd seen a crowd of them at a funeral once. "Why is it here? Oh, wait. Is that Director Abroft?"

"He just said Ekki."

"I'm Abroft." The creature's voice was soft. "Wasn't I expected?"

"Not entirely, but okay. I'm ready for breakfast. Why don't we talk in the kitchen."

The two followed her to the back of the house. Ruby went to the fridge. "I was going to have leftover takeout Thai. Danno, if you want something different, help yourself."

"I'll have what you have." Danno sat at the counter. There was a bowl of cherry tomatoes there—Abroft reached for it, then gave her an enquiring look. She signaled him to go ahead.

Danno looked into the cardboard containers and carefully scraped out some prawn fried rice. "Where's your uncle?"

"He's sick with the flu."

Danno frowned. "He's in the hospital?"

"No, just staying in bed." She turned to Abroft. "He said to go to the meeting without him."

"But—" Danno began, then hushed up when she gave him a warning look. He shrugged and picked up another take-out box.

"How are we to travel?" The wibble popped a tomato into his mouth.

"Captain Urbana's supposed to pick me up here in an hour. I thought she would get you at your home, though, not for you to come here. I'll text her you're here in case she thought so, too. How did you even get in?"

Danno took his filled plate to the microwave. "I let him in back."

"I told you not to answer the door."

His hand paused over the microwave controls, then stabbed a button. "You said if the doorbell rings, don't answer. He knocked."

Ruby rolled her eyes. "Don't answer the door no matter what."

Danno turned red. "Okay. I can go outside, though, right?"

"In the back yard, if you stay out of sight."

When the microwave dinged, he took his plate, grabbed a fork from the counter, and went out the back door. Director Abroft watched him leave, then turned to Ruby. "I think he's angry."

"Yes, I'll talk to him in a minute." Ruby scooped out some fried rice for herself. "Did you get a copy of Captain Urbana's notes about the Skohlars?"

"Yes, but I haven't had much chance to look them over. I brought them along, so if there's some time before they arrive…?"

"About an hour, like I said. If you want to talk about it, I can in a little while."

Ruby heated her food a little—she didn't like it really hot—and went out back to look for Danno. He was seated on the step of the gazebo.

He gave her a look that was hard to interpret and shifted aside to make room. "Ekki is adorable. I wanted to hold him."

She sat. "That fur does look awfully soft. But he's a person, not a cat."

"I get that." They were quiet for a while, then Danno set his empty bowl aside. "I know Simon isn't in his room. It's not nice to lie."

Ruby finished the bite she was chewing. "It's not nice. But sometimes you have to."

"Why?"

"Suppose you see a girl hide. Then a man runs up holding a gun and asks you, 'Where did she go?' He's really angry. Do you show him where the girl is?"

Danno looked worried. "He might shoot her."

"Right. It's better to lie than let him hurt the girl."

"Is someone trying to shoot Simon?"

"No, that was just an example. I'm not supposed to tell why, but a lot of people could get hurt."

Danno pondered this for a moment. "Ekki won't hurt anyone."

"We can't tell anyone. You just have to trust me on this."

Danno shrugged irritably. "Okay, but then I won't come in until he leaves. I'll stay outside and weed."

"Please also pick anything that looks ripe. Do you need me to tell you the list of repairs inside?"

He looked at the ground. "No, I remember."

Ruby put a hand on his wrist. "I know it's hard for you with your mom away."

He shrugged. "She'll be back."

"Yes. We know where she is, and she's doing what she has to, to keep you." She stood, wiping her hands on her jeans. "Remember to write down your time so we can pay you, okay?"

Ms. Wheelwright had gone back to the hospital for more tests, giving Olga a chance to clean her room at dawn without having to run into the cops who were guarding her. As she was in the private bathroom rinsing her cleaning rag, she spotted the intruder through the window. At first she just noticed a bit of movement, but when she moved closer to look, hoping to see one of the elusive gardeners, it turned out to be a strange man instead.

It was a sandy-haired, skinny white man in a green track suit, keeping shrubbery between himself and the house. He looked around and up—Olga ducked back to avoid being spotted. He ran to crouch behind the gnome den.

Dammit! They'd just taken the house off of lockdown! Olga threw the wet rag into the lavatory and ran downstairs. William was in the conservatory, feeding the cats. He frowned at her. "You can't be done tidying that room—"

"No time. There's a strange man in the garden."

Ithikate was just coming out from the hallway—she froze for a moment, then turned herself sideways and rolled at full speed the way she'd come. William stood, in no particular hurry, holding one hand to the small of his back, and held the empty cat food can away from his suit while cats swarmed around his ankles. "Where exactly? Describe him."

Olga told all. William stepped carefully over a calico toward the French door to the garden. "I think I know who it is. Please telephone the police. I, meanwhile, will keep an eye on him. One moment, though."

Olga, who'd been on her way out, backed up.

"You have a smut on your cheek, just there." William brushed a thumb against his own cheek. "Let's be spic and span."

As she reached the phone, the lockdown alarm sounded—everyone was going to love that. She took Derek's business card from her pocket and dialed his cell. While it rang, she licked her thumb and scrubbed at her cheek, then looked at the thumb—clay. She must've touched her face while working in the pottery studio.

"Detective Garbers. What's up?"

"There's some guy snooping in our yard. This is Olga at Ms. Wheelwright's."

"Yeah, I got caller ID." A pause. *"Look, I'm not nearby. Is this something a regular officer can handle?"*

"I guess. Everyone's hiding, anyway."

"I'll call it in, and someone will come, but there's probably a plainclothes officer out front keeping an eye on the place, so you could speed things up by running out to open the gate for him."

She pushed the gate button on her way out the door and ran up the drive. After the cool indoors, the summer heat was like being smothered under a moist rug—it was real easy to get used to air conditioning. She ran out onto the sidewalk just as a muscular woman in a beige suit came walking briskly from down the street, reaching into her jacket pocket to show a badge in a black leather wallet. "I got a call—"

"Yeah, in here." Olga led the officer around the side of the house, where they found the prowler on his knees, one arm inside the gnome home up to the shoulder, while William, with a two-handed grip on the seat of his tracksuit, tried to pull him away.

"Get offa me!" the stranger yelled at the the top of his lungs. "I saw 'em, and I'm gonna catch one!"

The officer stepped up and showed her badge to William. "Sirs, I need you two to separate. You, on the ground, I'm a police officer. Stay down there and don't move."

"Grab an edge of this and help me move it! There are little men in here!"

The gnome home was a gigantic pottery dome shaped like the bottom half of an onion. Extremely solid, it must weigh at least four hundred pounds, and probably it was anchored besides. No wonder he couldn't move it alone.

"Sir, I'm not kidding." The officer grabbed the wrist he was using to hold himself up and dragged it behind his back. He went down cheek first onto the gravel path—that had to hurt. "I said don't move." Keeping a hold on his wrist, she dragged him away from the dome.

"Ow, leggo!"

She looked at William. "Who are you?"

"William Fitzmorgan. A member of the staff."

"Do you know this man?"

"He was here once, the other day. He lives next door." William pointed. "Or so he said. He called himself Rex Edmunds."

Ah. This was the croquet ball neighbor Marissa had told Olga about. Could his appearance here now be something more to do with Marissa's power?

The cop took a firmer grip on the man, who was still trying to roll away. "Does he have permission to be here now?"

William crossed his arms. "He does not."

"You've got to listen to me." Edmunds pointed at the gnome dome. "They've got creatures! Just look in there if you don't believe me."

She sighed. "I swear, I get at least one of these every day. Sir, is there some medication you're supposed to be taking?"

"Look for yourself! Little people. Little, tiny people! They don't even come up to my knee!"

"There's no ordinance against little people, so they aren't my concern. However, I'm bringing you in for trespassing and resisting arrest."

"I'm not resisting!"

"You can argue that later." The officer produced a zip tie from somewhere, leaned over to grab his other wrist, and in a flash had his hands secured. She hauled him to his feet and handed William a card. "If you want to press charges, I'll need a statement from you. My number's on there." She pushed Edmunds inexorably toward the street. "You, sir, have the right to remain silent, and I wish you would. You have the right to an attorney...."

Olga followed them to the street to get the gate. It then occurred to her that she should walk the rest of the way around the house to check for other intruders. She continued around the north side, through the shade garden, and past the shed where presumably mowers and such were kept. As she checked the padlock on the shed door, William came into view from the other direction. "All clear," he said.

"I thought we had motion detectors and stuff along the fence."

"We do. I'll ask Margo to look into why they failed to alert us."

When the van pulled up to take them to the negotiations, Director Abroft was waiting with Ruby in Simon's drawing room. She hurried him outside, wrapped in a concealing cloak. It was one of several, of different sizes, kept in the front closet for that purpose. She frequently wondered what the neighbors thought went on at their house, with the mysterious comings and goings.

They weren't likely to guess.

Inside, in the back seat, Abroft shed the cloak. Ruby took shotgun, and Urbana twisted in the driver's seat to look in back, then at the house. "Where's Simon?"

"He's ill," Abroft said, "and will stay home."

Good, maybe Ruby wouldn't have to lie to Urbana, whose constant suspicion of her, to be fair, wasn't completely undeserved. She was much more likely to believe Abroft.

Urbana shrugged and put the vehicle in motion. Dr. Sin patted his lap, and Abroft gave a little peep—of joy?—and climbed onto it. "Where do we meet?" He reached up to clasp Dr. Sin's collar and looked out the window at the passing scenery.

"We've set up a neutral space." Urbana glanced up at the rear-view mirror. "We've met there before."

The ride wasn't far. Most of the Skohlars must live in the inner city, with its many sub-basements, sewers, and forgotten spaces. They pulled up in a tiny parking area, just two spaces, off an alley behind a grimy commercial building. Urbana got out, reached up to grab a hook projecting from the brick wall, twisted it, and pulled out the brick the hook was attached to. She fished in the opening for a key, used this to unlock a rusty metal door, then held the door open with her foot while replacing the key and the brick.

Dr. Sin had meanwhile gotten out of the van and opened the rear doors to remove a large wicker basket. He handed this to Ruby—it was fairly heavy—and motioned them to follow him through the door. Abroft scurried after him, Ruby followed with the basket, and

Urbana came last. The space just inside was a stair landing, dimly lit by fluorescent bulbs in cylindrical cages.

Urbana replaced the key and eased the door shut. "Remember, Ruby, you're just here because they want you present. Pay attention to the negotiations in case they ask your opinion, but don't speak up otherwise. As far as I'm concerned, you're here to listen."

Everyone seemed to think she was just there for show. But this was important stuff going on. If there was danger the Skohlars's goings-on could expose everyone, they had to work things out.

They didn't think she was capable of doing more. Well, she'd just see about that.

They descended two floors, into dampness and mustiness, until the stairs ended at another locked door with a number keypad. Dr. Sin bent over this, using his phone as a flashlight, and they were through and into a short hallway with three doors. The air here was fresher, the lighting brighter.

Dr. Sin pointed. "Bathroom there if you need it." He passed through a different door, into a large conference room. Ruby set the basket on a table near the wall and looked around the room. It was dominated by a large, scarred conference table. Around the table were ten or so metal folding chairs painted with tan enamel, dark metal showing through the chips.

Captain Urbana bent over the basket, removing its contents to set on the side table—a stack of flat cushions, paper cups, two cardboard cartons with spigots, and a flat white box that might be from a bakery. She picked up the cushions and threw one each onto four chairs, two on each side of the long table, near the far end.

Dr. Sin caught Ruby's eye and held up a paper cup. "Do you drink coffee?" He touched a spigot box. "The other is hot water for tea."

"Coffee, if it's not decaf. Thanks." She watched him fill three cups and investigated the white box, which did contain baked goods. She took a croissant and a napkin and chose a seat.

The end of the table opposite the door was cordoned off with a little wooden railing about six inches high, behind a small speaker. There was no chair at the end but a wide, steep ladder of closely-spaced white wires from floor to tabletop. On closer inspection this turned out to be a shelf from a modular shelving unit. She'd once had some like it in her closet.

Urbana sat, set down her cup and a donut on a little paper plate, and reached for a button at the middle of the table. When she pressed it, nothing happened, but she seemed satisfied, opening her attaché case and removing a notebook and pens. She glanced up at Ruby. "So. Any word about Spider?"

"Not ye—um. Were we expecting to hear from him?" Face of innocence. Face of innocence.

"I understood he was overdue with an important cargo. Simon called your friend Melinda to ask about it, apparently moments before illness struck him down. So suddenly."

Ruby carefully didn't look at Dr. Sin, who was just seating himself opposite her. "Not Melinda, Marissa. Simon doesn't tell me everything. Why were you talking to her?"

"I wasn't. I heard it from Ms. Wheelwright's secretary. She was concerned because the Sasquatches asked her where he was. Everybody's wondering what happened to Spider. If there's a problem, why hasn't anyone called me directly?"

"Maybe because there's *not* a problem. Maybe the Sasquatches have heard from him." Ruby took a careful bite of her croissant, holding the napkin to catch flakes of pastry. It was light and buttery, and the coffee was actually not bad either. "So they didn't need to call you. What?"

"Why don't I believe you?"

"I've often wondered that. I don't always obey you, but I don't think anything I've told you has turned out to be a lie." At least, not that Urbana could prove. "And yet, you never believe me."

Dr. Sin waved a hand to get their attention and pointed past the end of the table.

Ruby leaned over to look. A section of baseboard had swung up, and a line of Skohlars emerged. First out was Crunchy Bits O' Cheddar—"The Cheddar" for short—the Skohlars's leader. He was recognizable by his opal-tipped scepter, gold-embroidered vest, and by the dark markings over his eyes that made him look perpetually surprised. Following him, a young light-colored female wearing a Barbie backpack, also familiar. She was the smallest in the group, maybe nine inches not counting the tail. Then an older female she didn't know, with pearl earrings and a pearl-edged black velvet vest, a couple of important-looking older males, and a young male with a sort of saddlebag whose pockets contained a tiny spiral notebook and some pencil stubs.

This was apparently her day for dealing with people without pants because as usual, the Skohlars's only clothing was their vests. The delegation swarmed up the shelf-ladder and gathered behind the little railing, the one with the Barbie backpack hurrying ahead to plug a wire into the speaker and set a tiny microphone into a bracket mounted on the railing. The Cheddar reared up to lean on the railing, waiting for Barbie to flip a switch and adjust a knob on the speaker. She nodded to him, and he leaned over the microphone.

"Let us begin." He looked around at them all. "First, I am pleased you met our demand to bring Ruby. Wild Caught, show me the notes from last meeting."

That was all the greeting she was going to get, apparently, and Abroft was being ignored entirely. Skohlars weren't big on pleasantries. The saddlebag Skohlar, who must be named Wild Caught, presented the Cheddar with the little notebook, open to a page midway through. The Cheddar set it on a ledge behind the railing, and the other older Skohlars clustered around to look. The Cheddar covered the microphone with his paw, and the four of them conferred for a few seconds before he again spoke into the mic. "We considered your request for a map of our tunnels. No."

Dr. Sin said, "We understand your need for secrecy. We don't need a complete map, only the locations of anything we should steer people clear of, in case someone decides to excavate where you have something important."

"Only say where important things are?" The Cheddar gave a little double head-toss, which might be his equivalent of an eye-roll. "So more people can sneak in to sabotage them, like Sasquatch did? No. If someone digs, we notice in plenty time to move."

"Really?" Urbana said. "What if the city puts a new subway line through where you keep your arena monsters? You can move them on your own?"

The Cheddar exchanged looks with the other Skohlars. "You will stop them from doing this thing."

"We *can't* stop them unless we know what areas to protect before someone starts to dig." Urbana looked even more cross than usual. "We've been over this before."

And they went over it again, for two hours. Fortunately, Ruby had brought her sketch pad, so she used some of the time to draw the members of the Skohlar delegation. The young audio technician was the most interesting-looking one—her pointy, down-curved nose emphasized the submissive attitude conveyed by her body language, but she also had bright, active eyes that took in everything. Once when the Cheddar said something particularly dense, she started to do the double head-bob/eyeroll thing, then stopped and looked around to check whether anyone had seen it. Ruby gave her a conspiratorial grin, and she ducked her head, pretending to be busy with the speaker, which was working fine.

Once they had exhausted the topic of the tunnel map without any real resolution, the Skohlars took a break to huddle and talk privately, while the others stood, stretched, and went for more coffee. Barbie-backpack turned the speaker off and leaned against the railing, having nothing to do while the private discussion was going on.

Ruby didn't intend to let it be a private talk, though. She put her earbuds in and fired up Kirk's ultrasonic app, setting the phone near the railing in hopes of picking up some of the conversation. She did pick up some words, but they seemed to be just rehashing the same arguments they'd been having about the tunnel map. The lady with the pearl earring—Self Basting, Ruby saw from her notes—was in favor of giving them some information, and the others weren't agreeing but at least weren't talking over her or lecturing her. Skohlars might not be especially pleasant or moral, but at least they weren't sexist.

Ruby tore a corner off a sketchbook page and wrote a note on it—*What's your name?* She waved it in front of Barbie, who grabbed it and gave her a skeptical look. Grabbing a pencil from her colleague's pouch, which had been slung over the rail, she bent over the ledge to write an answer.

Minty Goodness. *Why you send me notes? I'm not important.*

Ruby flipped the paper over to write another note, smaller this time, to fit. *I think everyone is important. That's a pretty name. What do you do besides this?*

Abroft, returning from the refreshments table with a cup of fragrant tea, moved closer to watch. "What are you doing?"

"Trying to make new friends. That water can't still be hot enough for tea."

"It is, though. I think there's something special about the boxes."

Ruby went for a coffee and donut. Urbana and Dr. Sin were having their own private consultation at that end of the long table, heads together over their notes. When she returned, a reply from Minty was waiting. *I take care of my ten pups. Do you have any?*

"Ten!"

The Cheddar, from his huddle, gave her an annoyed glance. She waved an apology at him and looked closer at Minty. She looked young to be a mother. And so many! But rats had large litters—maybe Skohlars did too. Using a plastic knife that had been in the basket, she cut off a small piece of donut and set it on the railing, where Minty immediately picked it up and began to nibble at it. Ruby wrote another note on a fresh strip of paper. *No, and I never want any. How old are yours?*

The Cheddar and his advisers, or whatever, were still talking, Self Basting arguing they should tell the humans about the frozen soldiers. The what now?

"They scared away our helpers," said the old female. "We need their help if we ever have to move the lab."

The Cheddar looked at her, narrow-eyed. "Our people can do anything when they work together."

Self Basting shook a front paw for emphasis. "Not fast enough to keep them frozen. They cost much to replace."

Ruby glanced at Minty, who was holding their notepaper down on the railing with one paw and looking at her suspiciously. Minty looked at where Ruby had been looking, at the group of Skohlars. and walked over to them. She touched the Cheddar's foreleg, and he bent his head to listen. He then gave Ruby a long, considering look and ushered the group to the far side of the table. They resumed their conversation too low-voiced for Ruby to hear. Minty returned to lean on the railing, swinging the note from one paw. "Some three months. Some six months," she said. "That's how old they are. It's rare for so many to survive culling, but they are smart like their mother. We breed for that now." She pointed the folded paper at Ruby's phone. "This is how you hear us?"

Ruby sighed. "Yes." Abroft was apparently absorbed in his binder, but she didn't want to say more where he could hear. She pulled the note gently from Minty's grip and shielded the paper while writing, *I won't say anything about the frozen soldiers, but I want to talk with your boss in private.* She passed it back and sat back to wait for the next boredom session to begin.

Simon tried to do to some work. He had a long list of paperwork tasks that had been piling up for clients who couldn't or wouldn't write, and given that he had to wait by the phone anyway, it was a good time to do them. But he couldn't focus.

The third time he rose to pace in front of the window, the Sasquatch elder, Karomeenut, set his book aside and frowned at Simon. "Can you not keep thtill? You dithtract me."

"Why don't they call?"

"You might try meditation." The couch creaked as the Sasquatch stood—specially made with steel reinforcement, it was stronger than its spindly legs suggested. He stretched and walked over to the wall to replace the heavy, leather-bound book on its shelf. "Be calm. They will call."

"They said eleven. It's ten after now. It's unprofessional. Makes me nervous, too. I wish we'd been able to bring in a professional hostage negotiator."

Karomeenut shrugged. "Often the experth we need are not available. Thecrecy ith a burden. I'll make more tea."

"Eh? Oh, sure. I'll have some, too."

The Sasquatch started for the door but paused when the phone rang. Simon strode over to his desk. "No caller ID." He stabbed at a button on the recorder, missed, tried again, then pressed the speaker button on the phone. "Yes?"

The voice that came from the speaker sounded artificial, electronic. Obviously disguised. *"Do you have my money?"*

Simon looked at Karomeenut, who gestured at him to go ahead. Simon leaned over the phone. "It's going to take a couple of days. It's not easy to get together that much cash without attracting notice. This would be much simpler if you'd take CryptidCoin."

"No, I just don't do that. Cash or no deal. No fairy-geld either—I know how to tell. You have one day. I'll send instructions by email."

"Just a minute. We have conditions."

"You're in no position to make demands."

"We have to know you can deliver on your end. Are you holding the… *cargo* in the truck? It will damage it to keep it confined for long."

The Sasquatch, looming over the desk, clenched and unclenched his huge fists. "You will break them."

"I know what I'm doing. They'll be fine for another day or two. You can save them by hurrying with my money."

Simon raised a hand to stop the Sasquatch from speaking. "We need to speak with Spider. You have to prove he's all right, and he needs to assure us the cargo is intact."

There was a pause. *"He's fine. The cargo, as you call it, is fine."*

"We have to hear that from one of them or no deal."

An even longer pause. *"You can talk with Spider, but not right now. I'll call again in three hours. Get the money."*

"Wait!" Karomeenut lunged forward, but the kidnapper had hung up. "Damn them! Were they on for long enough to trathe the call?"

Simon stopped the recorder. "It doesn't matter how long they were on. This isn't a TV show. Let's see if they're stupid enough to be traced." He picked up the receiver and pressed a few buttons.

"Well?"

"What happened to being calm?"

Karomeenut gave him a dirty look.

Simon raised a finger, listening to the phone. Then he hung up. "No dice."

"We can't possibly haf the money tho quick. You can't thell art in a day."

"I'll call some folks who *do* take CryptidCoin and see how much cash they have on hand. And you can sell your holdings in Alavex."

"The taxes on that…." Karomeenut scowled.

Simon shrugged. "Unless you can think of another way."

"Feh." Karomeenut picked up his hat and gloves from the couch. "I'll talk with the otherth. Maybe we can find a better way to raithe the money."

"Will you come back to talk with Spider?"

He jammed on the hat and pulled out his phone. "I don't know. He ith your friend. I'm thorry we hired him now."

The negotiators left at about 12:30. As they climbed the steps to street level, Ruby hung back. Urbana, rounding a landing, looked back at Dr. Sin. "I'm starving. Want to grab a curry at Wow?"

Dr. Sin looked at his watch. "I can't, I'm afraid. Rain check?"

"Sure." Reaching the door to the outside, Urbana let them out, locked up, and hid the key. "Same time on Tuesday, then, everyone?"

Abroft waited by the door of the van. "If you still want me. I don't know whether I was much use."

"You didn't see them before. They're definitely a little more reasonable with the two of you there. You two study your binders, and if you have any ideas, email me." She slid back the van door. "All aboard!"

Ruby didn't move. "Actually, I have an errand to run around here. I'll get myself home."

Urbana looked skeptical. "You want to be left behind in *this* neighborhood? I wouldn't know how to explain that to Simon."

Ruby touched her Speck tube with the hand on which she wore a special ring Simon had given her. "I'm not defenseless."

"I'll walk with her," Dr. Sin said. "My next stop is actually not too far from here."

Urbana slid the door shut with Abroft inside. "Suit yourselves." She walked around to the driver's side, backed the van up, and waved to them before driving off.

"Thank you." Dr. Sin pulled out his phone. "I needed an excuse to get away from her so I could find out what's up with the Sasquatches." He held the phone up to his ear.

Great. Now how was she supposed to get rid of him? She pulled out her own phone, using the map app to find a plausible destination that was reasonably close.

"All right." Sin put his phone away. "We heard from the kidnappers. They'll call again at two. I need to get back to Simon's before then, and so should you. Will your errand take long?"

"Not too long, but the exact location is confidential. Walk me to Fifty-ninth, and I'll be fine from there."

Returning to the alley ten minutes later, Ruby got on tiptoe to retrieve the key and let herself in. Midway down the stairs, she found The Cheddar waiting alone on the landing, so she took out her phone and earbuds and sat on a step.

"So." He stood staring up at her. "You were spying on us."

"I was trying to find out what you really wanted. I won't tell the others about the frozen soldiers, but please explain them to me. Then I can help you figure out how both sides can get what they want."

"We have a right to defend ourselves."

Ruby shifted on the hard metal stair. "Of course. You also have a right to your secrets. But Captain Urbana and Doctor Sin don't trust you, and you're not super popular with most of the people who already know about you. So, if you're worried how others will react when you come out to The Scene, you have good reason. People are scared of you."

"And you will solve this?"

"I think I can help. Part of the problem is you're so secretive. People don't trust people who don't trust them. All the folks in The Scene have secrets, but nobody as much as you. The monster arena thing is another problem. If your people like violence, folks will think you're more likely to start trouble."

The Cheddar gave a little snort. "Your Guardian friend already ended that. We fight our last three monsters, then we are done."

"Yes, but it looks better if you end it on your own. Don't fight your last monsters. Send them back wherever you got them."

He twisted his head. "I tire of looking up at you. Sit here."

Ruby planted her butt on the landing, facing downstairs, and the Cheddar scampered up a few steps so their faces were level through the railings. "If we end the fights, we will fight each other. This is how we know which clan is to lead the others. My clan had the best monsters. Now, if someone challenges me, our clans will have to fight instead."

Ruby bit her lip. "These are complicated problems. To help solve them, I need to know your people better. Can't I visit? Talk with some of you?"

The Cheddar paced on his stair, holding his scepter by the opal knob like a cane, tapping on the rusty metal surface. "Very well, but not now. Come tonight, when my people are awake. We can talk more then, but I'm too busy to show you around."

"Could Hundreds of Uses guide me?" The old Skohlar had helped her investigate who'd released their invisible monster, and she'd grown fond of the grumpy rodent.

"No. She is dead."

It was like a punch to the gut. Ruby drew a ragged breath. "What... what happened to her?"

The Cheddar shrugged. "She was old."

And Ruby had hauled her around in a backpack through all sorts of jostling and peril, probably shortening her life. "Then... I don't know. What about Minty Goodness?"

The Cheddar nodded. "I think she's angry with you, but she will do as I say."

"Please tell her I'm sorry. I want to get to know her better."

"Tell her yourself. Come to the Monroe subway stop at ten. Meet at Adams end of platform." He tucked his scepter into the back of his vest and scampered downstairs, past Ruby, into the darkness.

Ruby looked past Marissa out the bus window, trying to see whether they were close to home. "Is this really gonna be okay? Didn't your folks tell you not to come over to our house?"

"It'll be okay because we won't tell them." Marissa clutched her giant black leather handbag to her stomach.

Ruby looked at her. Besides the cropped purple hair and all-black outfit, she'd added a little pewter skull pin on her vest. Ruby, by contrast, still wore the outfit Simon had picked out for her first day as negotiator—unbleached cotton top, beige skirt, and nice shoes. Compared to a few weeks ago, it was as if they'd traded places. "I think I'm a bad influence on you."

Marissa snorted. "Don't take too much on yourself. If my dad were reasonable, we'd get along just fine. Isn't this our stop?"

"Yes." Ruby stood, swinging her backpack onto her back. "Are you ready to rumble?"

When she let them into Simon's house, there were voices coming from the study, someone on speakerphone. *"...you know, with the melty top? Or some seafood—a clam repast."*

Marissa paused by the study door. "Is that Spider?"

Dr. Sin and Simon were hunched over the desk. A huge figure loomed behind them near the window, its face in shadow. Dr. Sin glared at them and made an emphatic shooing motion.

Simon was speaking now. "Once you're free, dinner's on me...." But Ruby had grabbed Marissa's arm and hauled her away, leading her to the back of the house.

"What's going on?" Marissa pulled her arm free. "Is Spider in trouble? Simon called me about him earlier."

"There's a problem, but I can't talk about it." Ruby opened the door to the basement and motioned Marissa to precede her. "They're handling it, and he'll be fine."

"That's less than reassuring. And what was that thing standing behind them? Are you working with cavemen now?"

"You've met Sasquatches before."

"Apparently not! I guess I saw one standing on your front steps awhile back. But they haven't come to Ms. W's while I've been there." Marissa looked around the tidy basement. "This is your martial arts practice space?"

"No, that's one level down. Stand here." Ruby leaned over to the wall to press the elevator switch, and Marissa grabbed her arm for support as they started to descend.

"That reminds me. How is Ms. W?"

"Hm?" Marissa squatted to get an early look at the subbasement as the ceiling rolled past. "Oh, she's home but still unconscious. She has a police guard, so that's probably a nuisance for the nonhuman residents. They also got a nurse from The Scene to look after her. This place is amazing!" She hopped off the platform before it came to a stop.

Ruby stepped off and sent it back up and went to the cabinet for her uniform. No practice swords today—it was basic forms again, so Marissa wouldn't be a total noob for her first lesson tomorrow. "Change into your fightin' duds, and I'll show you how it goes."

Marissa picked up the movements quickly, with Ruby to observe and correct her stance as needed. "You're a quick study."

Marissa grinned. "Thanks! I've been wanting to do something like this. When do I get to fight?"

"Oh, you want to hit me? Good luck with that." For a student of a few weeks standing, Ruby's confidence was high. "Ujo will decide when you can spar." She gave a secretive smile. "But if you like, I can show you a move you'll never see in the movies."

"Lay on, Macduff."

"Sorry?"

"Show me."

"Excellent, I've been wanting a human test subject."

"A what? Hey!"

But Ruby had already dropped into fighting stance, eight feet away. "Speck, tornado!"

She felt a slight breeze on her hand as Speck darted out of his tube and followed her pointing arm. Moving that fast, he wasn't visible, but Marissa obviously felt him hit and jerked back. But he was still on the move, bumping her in the shoulder, the back, the forehead. She backed up, batting her hands. "Make it stop!"

"Speck, tube." The tube thumped Ruby's chest as Speck flew back into it. "You're not hurt, are you?"

"Nice of you to think of that *now!*" Marissa kneaded her butt. "Not really, I guess."

"Good. He can hit harder than that, but it's supposed to just be a distraction. Okay, let's do eppy again."

Marissa adopted the stance. "I think you should tell me what's going on with Spider. He had a contract with the Sasquatches, didn't he? He was doing some work for them."

"What makes you think that?"

"At that dinner, he told me his contract was a 'big hairy deal.' Well, I just saw something big and hairy."

"Yeah, he shouldn't say stuff like that. Peppy."

Marissa shifted into the new position. "I noticed you didn't answer the question, though."

"I can neither confirm nor deny. Khaki."

Eight

This late, the station was nearly empty. The few passengers weren't especially curious, either, nobody paying any attention as Ruby wandered to the end of the platform to stare down at the rails. On the far wall was a sign that read, *"Danger - Keep Off Tracks — High Voltage."* When she'd met Skohlars on subway platforms in the past, they'd come out of the rail tunnel, so probably she *would* have to get on the tracks and would've been *considerate* of the CTA to indicate exactly where the high voltage was. Still, Minty, or whoever they sent, would know the details and wouldn't let her die. Probably.

She touched the tube on her backpack strap. Speck wouldn't tolerate being left behind after their recent separation. He'd obeyed her command to stay hidden during the negotiations, though. He'd killed a Skohlar the first time he'd encountered them, but she had trained him not to do that anymore. Hopefully. The Skohlars hadn't seemed especially fussed about the casualty, but even so, she really hoped he'd behave. "Speck, stay," she told him again.

She took out her phone and earbuds, fired up the ultrasonic app, and prepared to wait. But she'd barely settled herself on the last bench when a little squeak made her look up. A sleek head popped up over the edge of the platform and vanished again. Ruby wandered over and looked down at the tracks. No Barbie backpack, but the vest was blue polka dots on white, same as that morning.

"Do I need to get on the tracks?"

Minty did the head-bob of disdain. "The train people notice when people do that. You wouldn't fit the way I came, anyway. Pick me up, and I'll give directions."

"There's a padded tube in here for you to ride in." Ruby unzipped her backpack and set it on the edge, and Minty scampered into it. Ruby picked it up and gently settled it on her shoulders. "Where to?"

"Up a level."

Minty's directions led to an unmarked, rusty door in a shallow niche in a pedestrian tunnel. She emerged at this point, her paws cool on Ruby's shoulder, and held up a key. "Careful. It's dark, and there's a step down."

Ruby unlocked the door and slipped inside, feeling ahead with her foot for the promised step.

"Lock it, and hand me the key. I hope you had the sense to bring a flashlight."

"Yes, but I've also got something better." Ruby slipped out of the backpack and unzipped a side pocket to get a pair of sunglasses. She'd "borrowed" these from Simon's desk for nighttime monster stalking once before, and though they'd gained a crack across one lens during that adventure, they still worked. She slipped them on, and the darkness was replaced by sharp detail in monochromatic purple. She was in a smooth-walled, arched tunnel which descended at a gentle slope, curving out of sight. The ceiling was crowded with decrepit pipes and cables. Sections hung low where clamps had given way. "Oh. Unless you need the light?"

"I'm fine. Proceed."

There was only one way to go. As they descended, she tried to estimate how far below the street they were. Forty, fifty feet? They passed two other doors before reaching the end, a rough wall blocking the tunnel entirely. The pipes and cables were cut off at that point. She touched the hard surface. "Dead end."

"It's just a Dessin wall. Go on through."

"If Dessin means 'tons of concrete which nobody told me I'd need a sledgehammer to break through,' then yes, that's what it is."

"No, you can just walk through."

Ruby rapped on the wall with her knuckles—lightly because, yes, it was still solid and hard and rough. "Going to need more detail on that one."

"I'll show you." Minty scampered down Ruby's body to the floor, then walked into the wall, tail and all.

"Huh." Ruby knelt and felt the base of the wall where the Skohlar had passed, but it felt absolutely as solid as the rest.

"Are you coming?" Minty's front half had emerged from the wall a couple feet over.

"Still don't know how."

Minty did the head-bob of you're an idiot. "Just… know you can, and do it. See you on the other side." And she was gone again.

Was this a test? A puzzle?

If she couldn't see the wall, would it still be there? She took off the sunglasses, shut her eyes for good measure, and reached out. Still there. But Minty could walk through. She reached down again to touch where Minty had passed.

How was she supposed to "know" she could walk through when she plainly couldn't? Could she only pass if she was confident? How was a wall supposed to tell whether she was confident?

Still… Minty had passed through, so it must be possible. She leaned against it. *This is not a real wall. I can walk right through.*

The feel of rough concrete through her shirt was unfortunately very convincing. She took a step back.

Not. A. Real. Wall.

What if she convinced herself enough to make it partway through, but then started to doubt. Would she end up embedded in the wall? That was a horrible thought. But of course, if she made it partway through, that should be proof enough that she could make it all the way.

Not. A. Real. Goddamn. Wall.

She took a long, confident step and slipped into the wall, like plunging into cold water. Another step, and she was through. She let out the breath she'd been holding, checked on Speck in his tube—the regular little glimmer was there—and put on her sunglasses for a look around. Minty was ten feet farther along, at a connection to another corridor, this one with rails on the floor as well as pipes and cables overhead. She gestured Ruby to hurry and scurried around the corner. Ruby settled her backpack and followed.

The space they finally reached was farther down but not more than a couple blocks away—they must still be under downtown. The first hint was the smell—a musky, thick smell, like the world's biggest hamster cage, but without much of an overtone of urine. Then they rounded a corner into a large, irregular open space. It was a labyrinth of smooth, curved surfaces pocked with holes, dimly lit with improvised light fixtures. The space was supported by concrete pillars and sections of round tunnel wall or pipe that had been excavated around, leaving rough edges. The floor swarmed with Skohlars, with two wide passages crossing in a central area. Crosswalks and pipes also served as crowded highways between towers that might be Skohlar apartments, brightly painted lumpy constructions with balconies and round windows through which lights shone. The space was filled with noise, some she could hear with her own ears, some through her earbuds. Shouts, chatter, squeals, clatter. Skohlars paused to look at her, then hurried on their errands. Most were a little larger than her guide. All wore vests in a variety of colors, patterns, and materials, and a few had hats or jewelry.

It was hard to tell where individual sounds were coming from because she only had the one microphone, so it wasn't in stereo. But she could get some idea by pointing her phone in different directions to see which way was loudest. A lot of the nearby noise came from four Skohlars in a low-walled enclosure, fighting each other with sticks. They seemed to be pretty serious about it, and other Skohlars crowded the barrier, cheering them on. Farther away, a double row of open-topped stalls held traders with stacks of goods and others who swarmed around. And there, against the far wall, a team of three in black vests with steel studs seemed to be herding a line of—frogs, maybe?

She squatted down to talk with Minty over the noise. "Do you *all* live here?"

"No. This is the Clever Paw clan. Twenty thousand live here." Minty waved a paw. "There are many others in the city. But ours is the best place."

Twenty thousand. Ruby's old guide, Hundreds of Uses, hadn't known numbers that big. Minty also had a better vocabulary—she really was smarter than Hundreds. "How many clans in the city?"

"Thirteen."

This was good information that hadn't been included in the briefing materials. Did Urbana and the others not know about it? Ha! She got out her notebook and opened it to a blank page to start making notes. "Nobody seems surprised to see me. I didn't think there were many visitors."

"Your visit was announced. The Cheddar told them not to bother you. He was very clear."

"I see. Can I meet your family?"

Minty gave her a skeptical look. "You don't have to pretend to like me. I know you're just using me to get information."

"That's not true at all." Ruby put a hand on the floor to support herself. "Look, can you get back on my shoulder so we can talk without shouting?"

Minty grabbed her sleeve, leapt to her knee, and grabbed a ring on the backpack strap to finish the climb. Speck stirred, and Ruby motioned him back to his tube. She'd have to give him a little exercise soon if she could find a quiet place to do it—he got bored if left in there too long. Perhaps she should've tried harder to make him stay home, but it did feel safer to have him along, in case there was any kind of fight. She didn't think the Cheddar would try anything, and she'd left a note, anyway, in case she didn't return, but that wouldn't help her in the moment. She stood, careful not to jostle Minty, and held the phone up so the microphone would be near her. "Do I hear… singing?"

"Perhaps." Minty cocked her head, listening for a moment, then pointed. "Down by the water."

Walking carefully to avoid stepping on any tails, she threaded her way between the stalls toward the far end of the cavern. She got a lot of curious looks, but they didn't clear a space around her. They were so quick, they probably didn't consider her feet a serious threat. The shopkeepers looked apprehensive, since their piles of goods couldn't dodge, but she was careful to avoid crushing anyone's property, and soon they were in an open space that sloped down to a dark pool. A line of Skohlars headed for the shore carrying empty plastic pop bottles, while others rolled full bottles back toward the dwellings. Farther down, several Skohlars were hip-deep in the water, naked—their vests were piled on the shore. This was the source of the singing, which they did in chorus as they scrubbed something in submerged baskets, suds foaming up around them and drifting off into the darkness, away from the bottle-filling area. There must be a slight current here which kept the drinking water fresh. "That's a pretty song. I don't recognize it."

"It's new for me, too, but it sounds like it's by Just Desserts."

"I've never heard of that band."

"It's not a band. It's a composer."

It sounded like a Skohlar name. Ruby tried not to look surprised. After all, why shouldn't they be able to compose music? It just wasn't the sort of thing she'd thought would interest them. Plus, that was another thing not mentioned in the negotiation study guide. They really knew practically nothing about these people.

There were no words to the song, just "la" and "doop" and "fee," but done in harmony with little runs, some complicated timing, and a key change. "It's really good. Do you think they would mind if I recorded it?"

Minty waved her front paws, one up, one down. "Ask them yourself."

The washer-Skohlars looked at each other a little uncertainly when she made the request, but they were willing—even seemed flattered to be asked. It took a few minutes to set up, during which some curious water carriers clustered around. "Well," Ruby said at last, frustrated, "it looks like I can't record and listen at the same time. I'm recording... now. Please begin."

The singers had dragged their baskets onto shore, where they sat trailing suds into the water, and had donned their vests and lined up facing her. With the relevant parts no longer submerged, it was possible to see that they were about an even mix of males and females. They were also an assortment of ages. The oldest-looking one stood before the assembly and signaled them to start.

Ruby could see their mouths and throats moving but could hear hardly any of it. She hoped the sound recorder app on her phone was capturing the higher frequencies so she could fix the recording later. The group sang for about two minutes, then stopped and bowed as a group, while the onlookers slapped their paws against the ground, making the tiniest patter. Ruby restarted the ultrasonic app and thanked them.

"Now," Minty said, "turn around so they can undress and get back to work. The clothes don't wash themselves."

"Thanks," Ruby said again and headed back toward the bustling market area. "That was lovely. Do you sing?"

"Yes, but not silly doop doop songs. But the pups love Just Desserts, and they'll probably hear that song in school and sing it until I want to strangle them." Minty pointed. "Go to that tunnel. The Cheddar wants you to see the arena."

The tunnel was dark, so Ruby put her sunglasses back on. It was maybe half a mile long, a concrete tube, with many side passages cut into it, most too small for her. They eventually came to a heavy grate, wrist-thick bars embedded in the concrete. "Wait here," Minty said and climbed down, vanishing into one of the side openings.

Ruby looked at the space through the gaps in the grate. The room on the other side was huge, round, echoing, a junction with three other tunnel openings at irregular intervals. "Speck, go play." She pointed through the bars and took off her sunglasses to watch the little spark fly around. The space was otherwise profoundly dark, not a bit of light from anywhere.

Then there was a *click* from overhead, a *buzz,* and fluorescent lights in the ceiling came on, lighting a floor of fitted stone blocks, stained with what was probably the blood of past combatants. The walls were also made from large stone blocks with thousands of rectangular openings cut into them, each a few inches high by maybe two feet across.

There was a grinding sound from overhead, and the bars began to vibrate. Ruby stepped back as they rose, pointed ends rising out of holes in the floor. As soon as they were high enough to duck under, Ruby did so, walking out onto the arena floor. The wall openings, now that she could see the ones nearby, were blocked off with thick sheets of glass. Spectators must watch the fights from behind those. She peered into one—it went back farther into dimness—and what she could see was just a plain rectangular area, the floor covered with something crumbly, maybe sawdust. Skohlars didn't have a lot of use for chairs, evidently.

"There used to be enough space for everyone to watch at once." Minty was on the floor behind her, had probably come out of the tunnel while she wasn't watching. "But we're too many now. There are cameras for the others." She pointed up.

"Your people didn't build this space." Ruby waved at the huge room. "It would cost a fortune."

"That was long before I was born, but no, it was built by humans and held water once. There are other rooms like this one, but smaller, where the animals are kept. We open gates to let them in to fight."

Earlier that summer when a Sasquatch had sneaked into the Skohlars' domain and opened gates to let a monster out, it might have passed through this chamber on its way to the surface. It was lucky it hadn't gone the way she'd just come—the damage to the Clever Paw clan town would've been terrible, though most of the Skohlars were probably quick enough to escape into tunnels it couldn't fit into. "How did that Sasquatch know how to work your gates?"

"Since he's dead, we might never know. Most think he bribed a person who built them. They were not good bargain keepers."

Keeping one's bargains being the primary virtue to a Skohlar, this was harsh criticism. "Shocking."

"Everyone is very angry with them. If they return here, they will be sorry."

"If you tell Captain Urbana who they are, she'll take care of that."

Minty gave her a sideways look. "We can do it ourselves."

Pride—and also, maybe, they didn't want to give Urbana a chance to question the builders about any other work they might have done. Which reminded her…. "What about the frozen soldiers? Can you show me those?"

Minty gave her an evaluating look. "You would not fit. Recently we closed it up to humans."

To prevent further sabotage, presumably. "But what are they? Why are they frozen?"

"They are for if we need to fight. Someone made them for us and froze them until we need them."

"Made them? Like machines?"

"Grew them. They're… I don't know the word. They're Skohlars but tiny. Younger than pups."

"Embryos? You have frozen embryos? But why? If you need more baby Skohlars you already have, you know, a way to make them."

"Embryos," Minty repeated. "Embryos. Useful word. They are special. Not smart but strong. Larger. Obedient." She looked away. "I hope."

Genetically engineered warrior Skohlars. But…. "If you needed them to fight, they'd have to grow up first." And they'd have to find females to implant them in, but that might not be difficult.

Head-toss. "The Cheddar does not explain his plans to me. You can ask him this yourself when you see him later. Is there anything else you wish to see before you meet with him?"

"I really would like to meet your family. What else is there to see?"

"Wait for me in the passage while I turn off the lights. We can talk then."

Minty's pups were on the side of Clever Paw Town farthest from the reservoir in an enclosure with several hundred other young Skohlars, watched over by several old males with sticks. Minty whistled, and several of the pups stood on their hind legs to look, then hurried over to the barrier. When the rest saw Ruby, there was a commotion. The whole mob followed Minty's brood, their minders trying unsuccessfully to keep them in order with whacks of their sticks. One of the old Skohlars waded through the sea of excited pups to glare up at Ruby, then at Minty. "We can't have lessons if you bring outsiders to distract them."

Minty opened her vest to display a tiny badge pinned to the inside. "Official business. We won't stay long." She pointed to the pups in the first row. "These are mine. Imported Bavarian Hops. Red Dye Number Four. The others haven't passed their final tests yet, so they don't have names. Pups, this is Ruby."

"I like those names. Red Dye Number Four is kind of punk."

Minty sighed. "Dye names are a fad among her classmates. She'll be sorry later. I think people shouldn't be let to choose names until they're older."

"Do you like my vest?" Hops twisted to let Ruby see the garment, which was made of dark blue plastic liberally dotted with metallic gel stickers of stars and moons. The overall color scheme resembled his mom's polka-dot vest. "I made it."

"It's out of this world." It was also a little large, but he would grow into it. "They're cute. Who's their father?"

Minty looked at her blankly. "Why do you ask that? How should I know?"

"Oh, well I guess we do things differently. Humans, uh, keep track. Parents generally live together and raise their children together."

"Hmph. Must get awfully crowded." Minty pointed to the fourth pup from the right, a sleek, dark brown male whose vest was embroidered with zigzags. "You. Are you passing math next time?"

"Yes, Mother. And I have a name picked out."

"Great. You can tell me it later. Right now I am already getting a headache." She looked at Ruby. "Do you have any more questions for these miscreants?"

Ruby addressed the front row. "Did you learn any songs today?"

"Ooh, yes!" Red Dye piped up. "Just—"

Minty broke in. *"Not* by Just Desserts."

"Oh. We learned a new memory song yesterday. Do you want to hear it?"

What was a memory song? Ruby held up her phone. "I'd like to record it."

Minty looked at the cross teacher. "It wouldn't hurt them to practice, I think."

The teacher looked at the ceiling, as if to ask God why he sent these trials. "If you will leave after that."

"Okay, give me a second." After her earlier experience, switching the phone to record took only a moment. "Ready."

The entire crowd of pups sang, the teacher waving his stick to keep time. The other adults gathered in back to watch—they swayed in time but didn't sing. It was surreal to watch this all happening in silence, with several of the littlest ones obviously trailing behind at the end. The old teacher pointed his stick in a clear signal that they were to leave now, and the others started herding the youngsters back into their groups.

"Your pups are sweet," Ruby said once they'd moved away from the enclosure. "And smart."

"They're a nuisance, but it's my duty." But Minty seemed pleased. "The song was about the clans in Boston, their names and specialties."

"You're in touch with Skohlars in other cities? What do you mean, specialties?"

"Every clan has certain things they do best. In this city, for pottery go to Loose The Hounds clan. Tapestries from Brush. Like that."

Excellent info! Ruby pulled out her notebook. "What's Clever Paw's specialty?"

"Stealing."

And coincidentally the Cheddar, head of Clever Paw, was pushing back hard against anti-theft laws. "I'd like to see more, but it's pretty late for me so maybe on another visit. Is the Cheddar free to talk now?"

"We'll see." Minty pointed. "That way."

"Really, Red Dye is a fine name."

"We'll see. You know, this is probably one of the reasons the Cheddar likes you. You have a reasonable name with real, nice words. I ask you, what is a Chris? What is a Dreyfus? Ruby Park. With your name, you could almost be a Skohlar yourself. It sounds pretty."

"Uh, well, thanks."

"Have you been there? To the park?"

"Um, no. I'm not sure it's a real place." Explaining that Park was a common Korean name, rather than an English word, might be counterproductive.

The Cheddar kept her waiting for fifteen minutes. When he did show up, it was with a bag of potato chips, already opened, dangling from his mouth as he climbed to a little ledge opposite the folding chair she'd been told to wait in.

He took out a chip and held it in both front paws to nibble from the edge. "Fo." He swallowed. "So. You saw it all. What you think? How can we make the humans respect us?"

"Oh, is that what I was supposed to be doing?"

He waved the chip. "Certainly. They must regard us as equals. I will reward you for your help, of course."

Ruby held up a hand. "Hold up. I want to help you, but you can't give me anything. I'm on the other side of the negotiations, and it would look like you're bribing me."

"The trade has to be fair. You cannot help without payment."

She leaned forward. "Listen, uh, sir. This is part of my work for Simon, so I'm already being paid. Not much, I admit. The humans want you to succeed. If I help you, I'm already doing what I'm supposed to."

"I don't want to be in debt to the humans, either."

She closed her eyes for a moment. "All right. Tell you what. Send a gift to the delegates of the Scene, and we'll call it even. Send samples of the products of the different clans."

"Products?"

"The things they make. A set of cups from Loose The Hounds, a tapestry from Brush, whatever else."

"They will be too small for your people to use."

This just had to be a token payment so the Cheddar would feel free to accept advice, not anything really valuable. "That's okay. Is it a deal?"

The Cheddar shrugged. "Easy enough. Agreed."

"Then my advice to you is, you don't so much need them to respect you. You need the people in the Scene to like you or at least not fear you."

He looked at her narrowly. "But we are fearsome."

They would be excellent stealth assassins, but that wasn't the image Ruby wanted people to have, *at all*. "Right, you *are* fearsome, but you can also be friendly. Only those who mess with you should be afraid."

"We wish only to live in peace."

And steal stuff. Maybe not the best time to bring that up. "We need to make sure everyone knows you value peace. What you need is a PR person."

"What's PR?"

"Public Relations, but I don't know anyone who wouldn't, uh... I don't know anyone suitable."

"Why should they not trust us? We haven't threatened anyone."

"No...." Ruby thought this over. "But people are afraid of the unknown. Humans, anyway, maybe Sasquatches and the rest, too. They need to feel like they know you. You're so secretive, they wonder what you're up to."

The Cheddar made a little huff of exasperation. "So you would have us tell them everything? Give tours?"

"Not everything. I'm sure they all have their own secrets. Don't tell them about the frozen soldiers. I can understand your wanting them in case of emergency, but it would give folks the wrong idea. And, um, maybe not talk about eating the dead."

"Yes, I already told my people this. Who's been talking about it?"

"Retractable Blade, when I asked him what'd happened to the bodies of people the monster killed."

The Cheddar bobbed his head. "He is a brave fighter but not most clever. I'll speak with him again. It's silly, though. I myself have seen you eating part of a dead cow."

"You did? When? Never mind. The point is whether they can talk. Cows can't talk."

"None of them can after they die."

She wasn't going to win this one. "Whatever. It doesn't have to make sense. You just have to go along with it, and you already knew that, so good. Also, I get the impression something bad happens to pups who don't pass their tests. If *they* get eaten, I'd rather not know about it."

"Don't be ridiculous. They are still useful. We just do not allow them to breed."

Was that the truth? The Cheddar's expression was unreadable. Well, whatever. "I wrote down some other thoughts." She reached into her backpack for her notebook, but her hand found a different object. She pulled it out—the flat box containing the silver bells Ms. W had given her. "Huh. Um, actually…. Have you heard of reality TV?"

Marissa wasn't sure what woke her. McSchmidt was walking in the hall, his claws ticking on the floor, but he did that a lot. The street outside was quiet, and the clock on her nightstand said 1:30. She went to the kitchen for a glass of water and sat at the counter, looking out the balcony door at the moon in the little slice of sky she could see over the opposite roof. She played with her decoder ring, twirling the bands with her thumb to make them click.

She held up her hand, looking at the ring in the green light from the microwave display. It must mean something, but what had Ms. W intended her to do with it? But it wasn't like that, she knew. She supposedly—and Ms. W definitely—could tell what action would lead to the desired result but not exactly how. Still, she was supposed to use the ring somehow. To break a code? Who would be sending her coded messages? Some sort of puzzle?

Spider liked puzzles. And there was something mysterious going on with him. Still, Simon had been talking with him on the phone. If there was something he needed them to know, he could've just said it. What had he actually said? He'd been talking about food, hadn't he? But he'd used an unusual word. Repast.

"Paste," Marissa muttered. "Step. Pets. Spar. Star."

It hadn't been just repast. Some sort of seafood.

A clam repast. Spider was a weirdo, but that was still a strange way to say he wanted to eat clams.

She went back into her bedroom, McSchmidt following, and turned on her computer. A search brought her to an anagram website. She typed *Clam Repast*. Hm. Even if you only counted things that used all the letters, there were an awful lot of combinations. Still, a lot of them were nonsense. She copied off a few that might make sense as part of a message.

He'd said something else food related, hadn't he? Something that involved cheese. She leaned back in her chair and closed her eyes, scritching McSchmidt's head as she tried to recreate the words in her mind. Not just cheese. Melted cheese. On top.

But had he actually mentioned cheese or just said something about melting and she made up the cheese part?

Melty top. That's what he'd said. Or "a" melty top. Should she include the a?

She leaned over the keyboard and tried just "melty top." That made a lot fewer anagrams, and only one of them made sense as part of a secret message. She looked at the clock. 1:45. Too late to call. But if Spider was really trying to send coded messages in a phone conversation instead of just saying things, he might really be in trouble. Waiting might be a mistake.

She got her phone and called Ruby's number. That rang for a while and went to voice mail. She tried again with the same result.

She tapped the end of the phone gently against her desk. Ruby's phone might be turned off or on silent. Should she call the house phone? She might get Simon, and he was kind of grumpy and intimidating. But this might be important. She dialed the house phone.

It rang three times. *"Hello, Goodnight residence."* An unfamiliar boy's voice.

"Um. Who am I speaking to?"

"This is, uh, I guess I'm not supposed to say."

She rolled her eyes. That house and its secrets. "Where's Ruby? It's an emergency."

"I guess she's in her room. Wait, I'll get her."

There was silence for a minute, then the same voice returned. *"Uh, it's kind of weird. I can't find her room. It used to be there, but now it's a dirty attic, and there's no bed."*

"Her room is on the second floor in back."

"No, that's my room now. She moved upstairs. But I knocked on the door, and she didn't answer, and like I said, when I opened the door—"

"That's okay, I know what happened. But she should still be able to hear you if she's in there."

The boy seemed to be speaking to someone else now. *"I don't know, sir, it's for Ruby, but she's not here."* A pause. *"I don't know where she went. Okay, here."*

Simon's voice came over the phone. *"Who is that? Do you know what time it is?"*

"Marissa. I'm sorry to call so late, but it's important. It's about Spider. Is he in some sort of trouble?"

"I can't talk about—"

"Because I overheard a little of your phone conversation with him earlier, and I think he was trying to give you a coded message."

A long silence on the line. *"We can't talk about that on the phone. Are you on Signal?"*

"I don't know what that is, so no."

"I'll email you a link. Create an account and send me a connect

request. You can look me up with my email address. Going to my computer now." He hung up.

It took a few minutes to get things set up on her PC and connected with Simon. He had his camera on, and she could see behind him a file cabinet and a dimly lit wall with shelves of binders and curios. She'd never been in Simon's office, but this was presumably it. He wore striped pajamas and a bathrobe, and his own face was lit only by his screen.

"*What's the message?*"

Marissa pulled off the blue tape that covered her computer's camera. It seemed only polite. "Would it make sense for him to tell you, 'empty lot?'"

"*Hang on. Danno, go back to bed. I've got this.*" A pause. "*Okay. How do you get that?*"

Marissa explained her theory, then added, "And he said 'clam repast,' which is an odd choice of words."

"*I thought so, too, but figured it was just Spider being Spider. What does that unscramble to?*"

"Lots of things, unfortunately. I don't suppose the words 'scarlet map' mean anything to you?"

"*No.*"

"Anything to do with cartels, clarets, camels, castle? Last camper?"

"*Hm.*"

"Maybe if I could hear the whole message? And know what's going on?"

Simon sighed. "*Don't tell anyone. He's being held for ransom.*"

"He's *what?*"

"*Kidnapped. Along with some other people. He did say he had a bit of a view, so it's possible he was trying to tell us what he could see.*"

"So maybe he can see an empty lot! And…." She ran down her list. "A castle ramp? Some maple carts?"

"*That seems unlikely. Hang on, I'll send you the full recording.*" He leaned forward to type, the screen glow brightening on his face. On Marissa's end, a file transfer dialog popped up.

She put on her headset to listen to the audio file. This wasn't something her parents should overhear if they walked past.

SIMON: *Hello?*

ELECTRONICALLY DISGUISED VOICE: *You said you wanted to talk with your friend. Here he is.*

SPIDER: *Is it on?*

DISGUISED: *Go ahead. If you try to help them find you, I'll kill you.*

SIMON: *I hear you. Spider, are you okay?*

SPIDER: *They haven't hurt me. Sorry to intrude, pal.*

SIMON: *No problem. Are they treating you well?*

SPIDER: *Well, I'm under considerable strain. The accommodations are pretty poor, but at least I have a bit of a view. I can't recommend the food, either. I've been dreaming of a sandwich like you make, you know, with the melty top? Or some seafood—a clam repast.*

SIMON: *Once you're free, dinner's on me. What about your... passengers? Are they well?*

SPIDER: *I haven't seen them since we all arrived here, but I hear them bellow from time to time. I told these folks they need to be let out often.*

KIDNAPPER: *We know what we're doing. They'll be all right. Now you've heard what you need. Have the money ready by ten tomorrow. We'll send instructions then.*

That was all. Were there other clues in there? Anything unusual? Apart from being a call from a kidnapper, of course. She played it again, ready to write down any words that were possible clues. "Let me think about this and get back to you."

"*I'll stay by my computer.*"

Nine

S SOON AS they rounded the bend of the last tunnel, even before
the Dessin wall, Ruby's phone gave an assortment of beeps.
Bunches of missed calls and texts. Oops.

"I'd, uh, better get this."

Minty scratched at her ear. "Be quick. I have to lock the door
behind you."

"I can do it while I walk." She approached the Dessin wall, which
on this side looked even rougher and more convincing, with bits of
rebar poking out. She hesitated. "You first."

Minty gave a head-bob but scampered to the floor and vanished
into the wall.

Ruby breathed out. Okay. Eyes open this time.

It was hard to tell whether the wall dissolved in front of her when
she was an inch away or just got too close for her eyes to focus on it.
At any rate, it let her through, and there was darkness for a couple
seconds until she emerged, shivering. She looked down to make sure
she wasn't about to step on Minty, but the Skohlar was some distance
away, head cocked.

"Okay, I'm hurrying." Ruby worked the phone as she walked. Two missed calls from Marissa, two voice messages from Simon in the Signal app, texts from both of them, the last from Simon reading, *Where are you? Call immediately when you get this.* Crap. She used the Signal app to call.

"Where did you go in the middle of the night without telling me?"

"Hi, Unc. I'm with a client."

"Don't play games. You haven't been assigned any clients."

"But I have. You told me to negotiate with the Skohlars. I've just toured their city and talked with The Cheddar."

Silence on the line for a few seconds. "You got them to show you where they live?"

"The head clan, yes. I think I saw everything a human-sized person can reach."

Another pause. "There are so many things I want to say about that, I don't even know where to start. Come home immediately—we have a situation."

"What sort of situation?"

"I can't believe you think you can ask me questions right now. I am livid. Just get back here." He hung up.

"Trouble?" Minty asked.

She swallowed the lump in her throat. "Nothing I can't handle." She opened the door for Minty. "Thanks so much for showing me around. I think your pups are adorable. I hope they all pass their tests."

"I'm sure they will demand to see you again if you return. They're very unreasonable." Minty held up a key. "Lock it, then pass the key back under the door. Farewell."

Ruby followed instructions, pulled up maps on her phone to find the quickest way home by train, then decided "immediately" meant to use a taxi. She hurried up to street level.

When she got home she found a jeep parked outside and Simon, Dr. Sin, and a woman she didn't recognize in the study putting on equipment from piles on the desk. Bulletproof vests, ginormous guns, and bandoliers of oversized bullets. She stopped in the doorway. "What's going on? Is there a war on?"

Simon glanced at her, then went back to stuffing things into his pockets. "We have a location for Spider and the Sasquatches. We're going to get them."

Like Just Desserts, Spider and the Sasquatches would make a nice band name. She pointed at the tall, muscular, bronze-skinned woman in a tight-fitting t-shirt and khaki pants. "Who's this?"

The woman zipped her vest. "Salali Black."

Simon looked around, apparently deciding he had everything he needed. "She's a contractor from out of town. You stay here and hold the fort. If we need anything, we'll call. Three Sasquatches will meet us at the site. If anyone gets lost and calls you, the address is on this paper."

"Why such big guns?"

"These?" Simon held up his weapon. "Beanbag guns. Non-lethal. Also fairly quiet. Reggie, aren't you taking one?"

Dr. Sin held up his hands. "I will coordinate from behind the front lines."

"Take one, Colonel—you never know." Simon handed him an oversize pistol and leaned over his desk, opening drawers and pawing through their contents.

Ruby unslung her backpack and dug out the sunglasses. "Looking for these?"

Simon glared at her, took the glasses, and tucked them into a vest pocket. "Salali, you're driving. Let's move. Ruby, try to conduct yourself responsibly while we're gone."

She went to the door to watch them drive off, then shut and locked it. When she turned around, she found Danno sitting on the stairs, wide-eyed. He stood. "I was scared. So many people talking at once. The guns."

"They fight bad guys."

"I don't like fighting."

"Follow me." Ruby headed back toward the kitchen. "We'll make cocoa, then I have to call Marissa."

"Is that man really a colonel?"

Ruby got the mugs down. "I think that was a joke."

While waiting for the milk to heat, Ruby texted Marissa, *Home now.* Moments later the Signal app showed a call coming in.

"Where the hell have you been?" Marissa said.

She dug in the cabinet for the bag of mini marshmallows. "Everyone asks me that, but nobody waits to hear the answer."

"I'm waiting."

"Danno, marshmallows? No? Your loss. Sorry, M, can't tell you."

"Skohlars?"

Ruby raised her eyes to heaven. "Has Kirk been talking?"

"Of course he has. We don't agree with your silly secrecy rules. How come you can tell him but not me?"

How *had* that happened? It was a whole week ago. "I think he just happened to be there when I first heard about it, before I knew it was a secret. It's not like I go out of my way to inform him. He was just around."

"You hang around with him a lot."

She gave the phone a little shake and made an exasperated growl. "I thought we were past this. We're just friends, and he knows that."

"Yet you spend a lot more time alone with him than with me or the three of us together."

"Yes, because he can leave home when he likes without having to lie to his dad about where he's going. Plus you've been at Ms. W's a lot."

Silence on the line. *"I'm just getting angry. We should talk about this in person."*

"Okay, if you can arrive here a little early for the fighting lesson, we'll visit before Kirk picks us up."

"*What is he, your personal taxi service now? Wait, wait. Breathe. Never mind. I'll just see you then.*"

"Hey, wait! Don't hang up yet. I need to know what's going on with Spider."

"*Really, right now?*"

"Please, M. They were rushing out the door when I got here and didn't explain." She set the phone on speaker, got a spoon from the drawer to stir both mugs, and handed Danno's to him.

Marissa sighed. "*Fine. You remember yesterday I overheard part of a call from Spider....*"

Danno just sat at the counter and played with a metal puzzle from Simon's collection while they listened to Marissa's explanation. "*So, anyway,*" Marissa said at last, "*I figured he could see a vacant lot, a scrap metal dealer, and the Prudential building, so I looked in Maps for empty buildings with that view and only found one.*"

"Wait, you didn't say where you get Prudential from."

"*Intrude pal. It was the first match that came up on the anagram website. Now it's your turn to answer questions. Who's the boy you're alone with at ridiculous a.m.?*"

"Danno. We're just friends. He's... from Minnesota. I'll introduce you later. But how sure are you that you got the right place? I mean, maybe not everything you thought was a clue was a real clue."

"*Yes, I'm nervous about them acting on that. It's just a guess. Maybe he did mean maple carts instead of scrap metal.*"

"Or camel parts." Danno, eyes down, sipped his cocoa. "Or smart place."

"*Is that Danno, searching on an anagram website?*"

"No." Ruby looked at him curiously, but he'd gone back to his puzzle. "He came up with them on his own."

"*He's quicker than I am, then. I definitely needed the computer. Anyway, camel parts doesn't make sense, and I didn't find any carts, maple or otherwise, or castles. I looked for a Smart Place, but there's just the*

Smart Museum, and he couldn't be near there." Marissa lowered her voice. "*I should hang up. Someone's awake.*"

"Okay, meet you around one thirty at the dojo?"

"*Yah. Actually, no, now I check my calendar. Duh. We'll catch up after class.*"

Ruby tucked her phone in her pocket and leaned on the counter across from Danno. He looked up at her for a moment and frowned. "What? I'm not stupid."

"That's what I tell people. But I didn't know you were a word genius."

"It's just a trick." He gave the metal puzzle a final twist and pulled the ring off, holding it up. "Like this." He looked at her again, for about a second. "You're learning to fight, too? And your friend?"

"What? Oh, that. Yeah, we're taking a self-defense class."

"You have a gun?"

"No, and I don't want one. Our teacher talks a lot about how to avoid trouble. And the guns Simon and the others had are just to knock people out."

"They're loud, They hurt people. I don't feel safe. What if people come here with guns?"

"Danno." She paused. "Look at me."

He didn't look. She reached across and set a hand within his reach but didn't try to touch him. "I'm doing the best I can for you. This house is tougher than it looks." The cops had broken down the door earlier in the summer, but that would be a lot harder to do with the new doors, front and back. "We have another safe hiding place downstairs, just in case, besides the attic. Want to see?"

That got him to look up. "Okay."

"Finish your cocoa, and I'll show you. And then you have to show me how you got that puzzle apart because I couldn't figure that one out."

Ruby couldn't pace on the roof in her dream, and pacing was really optimal for an explanation like the one she was giving. But she could still gesticulate. "So I was like, you've got this huge arena, you've got cameras and mics in it, Skohlars are already set up to watch from home—not from their actual dens, but every clan has a couple of screens hooked in, and they gather around for the monster fights. So I told him, why not have the clans compete there, and everyone can watch?"

Micah nodded thoughtfully. "Kind of the rat Olympics?"

"Don't call them rats, okay?" Ruby shaded her eyes against the sun. "More like Skohlars Got Talent. They might have some athletes, but it's not so impressive to watch someone weightlift five pounds, you know? I mean, it might be impressive to them, but I want them to wow everybody. Their music is pretty good, and they're good singers. They also have musical instruments, though I didn't get to hear any on this trip. They'll do it elimination-style. Each clan sends their best group, and the judges eliminate one each week until there's a champion. I donated the grand prize, a set of musical bells. But the real prize is the winning clan gets status. It'll count toward deciding which is the next head clan."

"They're ready to come out to The Scene at the same time they start the competition?"

"I don't know, but it'll be recorded, so they can always share it later. I just think if this is the first thing people hear about them, it'll start them off on a positive note."

"No pun intended."

"Har har. It wasn't intended, actually. They'll have to move the cameras closer and build bleachers and stuff, since the performers are smaller, but they can do that themselves."

Micah shifted his umbrella to provide her some shade. "It sounds grand. I'm sorry I'll miss it."

She sighed. "Yeah, me too. That you will, I mean." She looked around at the surrounding rooftops. "It's always so damn hot up here.

Do you think if I build a shelter—like, on the real roof—it would be here in the dream, too?"

Micah chewed on his large lip, considering. "It might be hard to explain why you're doing it. Perhaps we could just imagine it. If we both try, it might happen. Oh, hey—you better answer the phone."

The phone. Ruby sat up, wiping at her face, and swiveled the desk chair so she could snag the receiver. "Goodnight Agency." And then, remembering, she looked frantically for the record button on the apparatus hooked up to the phone. If it was the kidnappers and she didn't record it, Simon would be even more pissed than he already was.

"It was a bust." Simon's voice, sounding disgusted.

Ruby relaxed and leaned back in the chair. "They were already gone?"

"They were never here. We scared the hell out of some old homeless guy, though. We must've misunderstood the clues. Anything at your end?"

"Not a peep."

"We'll have a quick look through nearby windows, just in case we got the almost right place, but expect us back in thirty minutes. If there were some sort of food ready then, that would be helpful."

"Early breakfast for four people? I'm on it, boss. Anything else?" But he was already gone. Ruby made a quick pit stop, then hurried back down to the kitchen. What sort of food would they want? She rummaged in the fridge. There were greens and cucumbers and tomatoes on the counter, but Salali hadn't struck her as a salad kind of girl. Deli meat and cheese. Eggs. Omelets were a possibility, but someone might prefer to grab their food and go.

She finally settled on omelet sandwiches. She took an armload of ingredients to the counter—turkey, provolone, mushrooms, spinach— and dumped it near the cutting board, went outside for herbs, turning on the coffee maker as she passed. Soon she had a pile of chopped ingredients and two skillets heating. There had been movement upstairs, so Danno would probably be down shortly. She added two more eggs to the bowl and picked up the whisk.

And that was when the doorbell rang. Damn. Who could it be this early?

"I got it!" Danno said, coming downstairs.

Ruby passed him in the hall. "You *don't* got it. Out of sight, mister. Go mix the eggs." If it was a creepy client arriving under cover of darkness, she didn't want to risk Danno's reaction, and if it was anyone else, she didn't want them to see him. She checked the peephole and saw the silhouette of a tall, wiry young man in tight-fitting clothes, pads, and helmet—a bicycle courier with a box tucked under his arm.

She opened the door a smidge, and he held out a tablet. "Sign here, please."

She scrawled her signature and exchanged the tablet for the box, which was over a foot square and four inches deep, heavy, with shifting, crinkly contents. "Hang on a sec." She closed the door, made a visit to the study for tip money from petty cash, and examined the box as she returned to the kitchen. It was addressed to her in big block letters. Well, that was odd. Who could need to send her something urgently enough to have it hand-delivered at five a.m.? Simon, or the agency, she could understand.

Danno had divided the eggs between the two skillets and was minding them. That was irritating, since she hadn't asked him to, but he seemed to have done everything okay. He must do most of the cooking at home—heaven knows Annie wasn't likely to do much—so it figured he'd know his way around a kitchen. Ruby set the package on the counter and carefully cut it open.

Several items, some packed in tissue paper. She pulled out a packet that felt like heavy fabric, a wad of bubble wrap sealed with way too much packing tape, a wide cardboard mailing cylinder. This gave a lurch as she pulled it out, and she barely managed not to drop it. Alarmed, she set it on the counter and stepped back. It rolled around, scrabbling noises coming from inside, then the endcap popped off, and a furry snout peeked out.

A Skohlar. Someone had mailed her a person. That was a first. The special delivery rodent came out, swiped his forelegs over his ears and shook his head, and adjusted his vest. He was light brown with black-tipped hairs, the vest was red velvet with gold embroidery, and he also had a tiny diamond stud on one ear.

"Retractable Blade?"

He gave a little bow.

"Hang on, I'll get my phone." She walked to Danno, who was looking at their visitor nervously. "It's cool. It's a client. You're doing great here. Can you toast some bread too? Four rye, four wheat, and whatever you want for yourself. It's in there."

When she returned, the Skohlar was eyeing the food still out on the counter. She glanced at the clock and checked on Danno, who was ready to turn the omelets. She took a little dish from the cabinet and inserted her earbuds. "Are you hungry?"

Retractable Blade glanced again at the food. "I could eat."

Ruby put a tidy pile of each ingredient on the dish. "How is it you come to be in my mail?"

"What?"

"Why are you here?"

Retractable Blade spoke around a bite of cheese. "The Cheddar sends me to say two things. First, I must say sorry for saying we eat people if they are dead. I don't know why I am sorry for saying a true thing, but the Cheddar says I am."

"I wasn't offended. It's just smarter not to mention it even if it is true."

Danno paused nearby, holding a stack of bread. "Are you pretending it's talking?"

Ruby raised her phone. "He's really talking, but I need this to hear him."

"I like his little shirt."

Retractable Blade straightened, brushing a paw over his vest with evident pride, and bowed. Danno blushed, lowered his eyes, and continued to the toaster.

"Also, I am told to explain all this to you." He waved a paw at the items scattered across the counter.

"These are products from the different clans, right? I didn't expect them so soon."

"They come from the Cheddar's own trove of tribute gifts. They are the best from each clan."

"Please tell him I'm honored he sent such fine items." Ruby extended a hand. "Climb up, and let's go where there's room to spread things out so you can tell me what's what."

When the raiding party returned a few minutes later, there was no longer any sign that rodent feet had trod, however briefly, on a food preparation area. The dining table was spread with the contents of the package. Retractable Blade sat on a high stool to eat while explaining each item, and Ruby took notes. On entering the room, Simon paused, then moved aside to clear the doorway. "What's going on here?"

Ruby waved to Salali, who stared at the Skohlar as she passed. "I had a very, um, productive talk with the Cheddar last night, and he sent us gifts. Look at this tapestry, isn't it pretty?" She held it up, waggling it back and forth. "See? 3-D effect. Thousands and thousands of tiny stitches."

Simon didn't look at the tapestry. "I still can't believe you went down there."

"I'll tell you all about it later. You must be hungry." She waved at the spread on the bar counter. "Sure smells good."

"We'll have a *long* conversation about this later, but yes, there are other priorities at the moment."

Dr. Sin put on reading glasses to examine a tiny pottery cup. "Skohlars made these?"

"All these things. There are clans with different specialties, and the Cheddar sent samples from each." She remembered Clever Paws' specialty and amended, "Anyway, from those who make things."

He slid open a tiny door in a lacquered triangular cabinet. "It's like a tansu." He carefully unfolded a soft vest with an overlapping scale pattern of multicolored feathers. "Silk lining."

Retractable Blade pointed to another item near the vest. "The cap goes with it. Maybe I will have a suit so fine when I am too old to fight. Twin Pack of Brush clan made it."

Ruby passed on this information and added it to her notes. "So you raided the wrong place? What's the next step?"

Dr. Sin looked at the Skohlar and at Danno, who ate eggs on a half bagel while gazing with adoration at Salali, who ignored him. "We'll discuss that in privacy." He stepped toward the food, then paused and looked back at Retractable Blade. "I have an idea. Ask him if he can stay a couple of hours."

"You just did."

Simon walked past with a plate, beckoning to her. "With me. Reggie, we'll talk in a few minutes."

Okay, so this was trouble coming down on her. At least the package from the Cheddar could hardly have been better timed, since she now had something to show from her excursion. But Simon definitely had an angry-looking back. "You know," she said, "we really should get another pair of those sunglasses. Another few, since the one is cracked." She laughed, but it came out more like a gurgle. "So we'd have a spare."

He passed into the study without holding the door open behind him, and she had to bump it open as it swung shut in her face. Simon sat behind his desk and motioned her to a chair. Once she was seated, he studied her in silence for a little while. She put her hands under her thighs and shifted in the uncomfortable chair. It might be an antique, but it wasn't—

"So." Simon put his hands flat on the desk. "You took it upon yourself to go out in the middle of the night without telling anyone."

"And it worked out really well."

"Into a potentially hostile environment."

"Me and the Cheddar are simpatico." She held up two fingers together. "We're like that. He wouldn't hurt me. Anyway I left a note."

"Yes, I found the note. That is, however, not exactly the same as asking permission."

"If I'd asked, would you have let me go?"

"By yourself? Of course not."

"That's what I thought. But they weren't about to let me visit *not* by myself. So you see, I had no other way to get the vital information we need."

Simon's jaw clenched. When he spoke, it was with more precise enunciation than usual. "Since you can apparently predict what I'll say if you ask me, then if you know I'll say 'no,' I'd like you to take that as a 'no.' If you're in any doubt what my answer will be, of course, feel free to ask."

"But—hey, wait! I found out lots of things we needed to know for the negotiations."

"Let me think how to put this." Simon leaned back in his chair, bumping his tented hands against his chin. "All right. Are you familiar with the term 'Russian Roulette?'"

"I've heard it, but…."

"It involves a revolver loaded with one bullet. You spin the cylinder, so there's a one in six chance there's a bullet in the chamber. Now suppose someone says they'll give you a thousand dollars if you put that gun to your head and pull the trigger. Is that a good bet?"

"No."

"I'm glad you think so. But that's the bet you made last night. And here you are waving your thousand dollars in my face saying, 'See, I was right.'" Simon stood and walked to the window. "We're in a dangerous business, and we have to be smart about what risks we take. We have to make sure it's really worth it. Alasdair Polacek made a bad bet, and his family's paying for it. I would hate to have to go visit your parents in prison to tell them you'd lost your life for nothing. I'm sure whatever you learned from your visit will be useful, and I'm looking forward to hearing it, but we would've gotten there eventually. We're not in such a hurry to make a deal with the Skohlars that we have to put lives on the line."

"But didn't you do the exact same thing, going out monster hunting alone with your sword?"

"That's different. I know what I'm doing."

"I bet Polacek thought he knew what he was doing, too."

Simon returned to his chair, and did the hands thing again. "All right, that's a fair point. I'd gotten used to operating on my own, and it was a mistake to agree to the client's condition of total secrecy. I should've had backup. For this raid I got a group together, you'll notice, even though Salali doesn't work cheap. I'd like you to use that as your model, not my earlier reckless exploits. Okay? We're a team now."

Ruby sighed. "I guess."

"I'm not saying we can't take risks. I'm saying we use our heads, and two heads are better than one. Think strategically."

"I said fine already."

"I have your word on it? No running off on your own without consulting me?"

Ruby held up her hands, little fingers linked. "Pinky swear."

"Good, because I was terrified when I found you gone. Don't put me through that again. If you weren't already using every spare minute learning the business, I would ground you or something. I should probably think of some other punishment. I don't know—I'm not great at this sort of thing."

"That's all right—I get it, honest. I'll be more careful. Please don't exert yourself."

Simon gave a half-smile. "And another thing. We can't just go out and buy more of those sunglasses at REI. I don't know whether I'll ever have a chance to get more pairs, so let's treat all the equipment with care, all right? It's like your Speck. You got him from that leopard woman, right? If you wanted another one, you'd just have to hope she shows up again."

Actually, she still had the paint and the crystal—she could create another mostly invisible flying dog. It's just that one was already a handful, and she wasn't sure how two of them would get along with each other. Still, she could see the point. "Okay. Sorry I cracked your sunglasses. I didn't expect to be in an explosion."

"Things happen. While we're on the subject of Speck, one question before the others come in. It looks like if we want the Sasquatches back, we'll have to deliver the ransom money. Naturally, we'd like to track it, but the kidnappers seem to know a lot about how we operate and about me in particular."

"So, it's an inside job?"

"Maybe. I'm afraid they might detect any tracker we tried to put on the money, and they'll certainly ditch the bag at the first opportunity. Is there any way you could get Speck to follow them and then come back and lead us to them?"

"Oh. Hm."

"Hm?"

Ruby shrugged. "He's great at tracking people once he knows them. That's why I originally got him, so I could track you down if you ever went missing on one of your solo adventures. But I've never trained him to track something other than a person, like in this case what, a packet of money? I'm not sure whether he could, and it would take at least a few days to teach him how. I mean, he's pretty smart for a dog, but...."

"We don't have a few days. All right, I'll think of something else."

"Where are we supposed to turn over the money? Couldn't we—"

"*We* aren't doing anything. You're going to your martial arts lesson as usual."

"You just said we were a team."

"And as soon as I'm satisfied that you can handle yourself, we'll do this sort of thing together."

"When will that be?"

"Probably when Master Ujo says, so keep practicing. Please go tell Reggie and Salali I'm ready for them."

Marissa hadn't gotten much sleep. Between staying up late in the first place, waking up to worry about Spider and puzzle out his message, worrying about whether he would be okay, then an early text from Ruby saying she'd gotten it wrong, then half an hour trying to figure out what she'd missed. Then, a text from Margo. *Priscilla is awake and would like to see you.*

So, summoned to the presence. Should she be honored? She already knew a phone call wouldn't do—security—and anyway if she went there, she could also find out from Olga what was up with the investigation. It could work with her schedule, provided she came up with a reasonable excuse.

She found her mom in the bathroom, putting her face on for work. "I have to shop for school. Clothes and stuff. Nothing from last year fits."

"On your own?"

"I'm supposed to meet Ashley and Sophie, shopping and lunch." She was still on the outs with Ashley since the birthday party swimming pool incident, and where Ashley led, Sophie followed, but her parents didn't pay close enough attention to what Mom referred to as "teen drama" to know that.

Mom glanced at her and picked up the mascara. "I was expecting you to watch Pablo and take him to softball."

Marissa's little brother was, in her opinion, old enough to mind himself, but her view wasn't popular in what in any case wasn't a democracy. "*Abuela* Cyntia can keep an eye on him."

Mom sighed. Cyntia was her dad's mom, and they didn't always agree on child-rearing methods. "Fine, but tell her no sugary snacks this time." Mom glanced at her watch. "I'm running late. Can you manage breakfast?"

"Sure, but what about your breakfast?"

"I'll pick something up at the coffeeshop." Mom leaned over for a smudge-free air kiss. "Love you! Remember, if any police want to talk to you again, you call your papa."

"Yes, of course."

Mom picked up her purse and checked its contents. "Make a healthy choice for lunch." She patted her own tummy. "Get into fighting form."

Marissa gritted her teeth but nodded briefly. After the door closed, she muttered to it, "I'm not fat. I'm pleasantly curvy."

It took another forty minutes to get out the door, followed by an hour on buses. She used the time to read about the latest LightSail mission. During the last block on foot from the bus stop to Ms. W's gate, she found her pace slowing. Her dread at returning to that place was unexpected, but now that she was near, she kept revisiting the scene of Ms. W as she'd seen her last, lying on the floor with William leaning over her as Derek ushered everyone else from the room to make way for the EMTs. And then the awful interviews which followed, the difficulty of trying to explain just how she knew Ms. W and why she'd been at the dinner in the first place to a detective who could obviously tell she was leaving things out, while her dad glowered in the seat beside her.

She reached for the keypad to open the gate, then let her hand drop. Her stomach was twisting up in knots at the prospect of going back in there.

"Did they change the code?" A hand reached past her to jab at the buttons, and Marissa whirled, heart pounding in her ears. It was Detective Derek.

"Sorry, didn't mean to startle you." He punched the final button, and the gate motor hummed into action. "Did they send for you, too? I understand the regular detectives already interviewed her. Listen to me, saying the regular detectives like I'm an old hand at this eerie stuff."

"You're a natural."

He paused ten feet up the drive and looked back at her. "You coming or what?"

She took a deep breath. "Yeah, okay." She stepped in and pressed the "close" button. "What do you hear about the case?"

"They're still looking at the cook as their main suspect, based on her having fled. Naturally, no luck finding her."

"Not a girl. Them, not her. I suppose it could be. I don't know them that well." Maybe this is why she was feeling so much dread at returning to this house. Chances were pretty good the poisoner was in the house, and she was waltzing right in. Not that they had anything against her. That she knew of.

Olga met them halfway up the drive. "We're on lockdown again. Someone's been sending drones over the wall. Margo has a thing to knock them out, but we want to make sure there's nothing for them to see anyway, even inside through the windows."

"Drones?" Marissa scanned the sky, but none were in sight at the moment. "Is it the police? But no, that doesn't make sense. Margo lets them in whenever they want, right?" She looked at Derek.

He shrugged. "I know the officer in charge, and he's no slouch. I'm sure he's aware there are secrets here. Of course, that's par for the course. Everybody lies to the police." If he'd ever been unhappy about that, he'd since gotten over it because he said this cheerfully. "If you show me the drones you've disabled, I can tell you whether they're department issue, but I doubt it. We don't have much budget for that sort of thing."

Olga opened the big front door and motioned them to go ahead. "Ms. W wants to talk with you first, Detective. Upstairs, third door on the right." She followed them in and pulled Marissa aside as Derek threaded his way between the exhibits toward the staircase. "What's the word about Spider?"

Marissa looked at Derek's receding back. Did he already know about the kidnapping? Was she supposed to say anything to Olga?

She was really starting to get why Ruby was always so reluctant to tell her anything. It wasn't so much that she didn't trust Olga— though, of course, their acquaintance was short—but the fewer people who knew a secret, the less likely it was to reach someone who wasn't supposed to know.

Olga stopped, hands on her hips. "I can see you know something. Are you going to tell me what's going on? The Goloopa's going crazy worrying about him. They go way back."

"I'm really sorry. I can't."

"Hell." Olga turned and walked toward the back of the house. "Well, I get it, I guess. But tell us when you can. Want to see what I've been making?"

"Sure." Marissa followed her to the basement door and down the stairs. This was a less fancy part of the house with linoleum, fluorescent lights, and plain drywall painted light green.

Olga stopped in front of the studio door. "My stuff isn't terrific yet."

"Since you've only been doing it for a few days, I wouldn't expect it. The photo you sent looked really nice, though."

Olga grinned and opened the door. "I can carve out slabs okay, but turning pots is tricky. I found some stuff on Videocricket, but watching isn't the same as doing, is it?" She went to a set of shelves where a few wobbly-looking vases sat, still a little wet. "The few sad survivors." She lifted a cloth cover to reveal more pieces, including the cat sculpture and others in a similar style. "These have to dry more. They'll probably break when I fire them, I expect."

"The sculptures all look great. And the vases… well, they certainly have character."

"I'm trying for a little less character, but thanks." Olga covered the sculptures and wiped her hands on her jeans.

"You've got a smudge of clay on your butt now."

Olga twisted to look. "Oh, yes! That's just great! It gets on everything, I swear!"

"I think there are aprons in that closet."

"I know about the aprons. I just forget to pay attention where I put my hands." Olga grabbed a paper towel from the dispenser over the big double sink. "Herself is probably ready for you by now. You go on, I just need to get cleaned up."

Marissa met Derek on the stairs, and he gave her a little salute. "She wanted an update on the investigation, but I couldn't tell her much."

She shrugged. Reaching the top of the stairs, she turned left, then paused for a moment to collect herself before entering Ms. W's room.

It was her first time in there. The place smelled of lavender and powder, the walls were painted deep purple with stripes of metallic gold, and the furniture was glass-topped tables and scoop shaped chairs—probably she'd bought them new in the 1960s. Two huge windows let in the morning light through filmy curtains. Ms. W was propped up in bed with a book and a lap table, and there was another person in the room, a plump, red-haired woman in a white uniform, knitting.

"Come here, child." Ms. W beckoned her closer.

Marissa stepped closer, glancing at the other woman.

"That's Maureen. Have no concern about speaking in front of her. I don't really need a nurse, but the police insisted I have a guard."

She very clearly needed a nurse. The left side of her face was a little slack, the eyelid drooping, and her hands shook as she set the book down. She looked tired and a little gray around the edges. "I think having a guard isn't a bad idea until you know who tried to poison you."

"Fiddlesticks. It's nobody still in the house. Sit down, you're making my neck hurt."

Marissa pulled a chair close to the bed and sat. "So you know who it is?"

"This is what those annoying police have been asking me until I sent them away. I can't remember any of it."

"But you know who was there, right? Why did you give people those presents?"

"I don't remember that, either. No matter, it'll come back, or it won't." She slid down a little, tugging the covers up to her chest. "Have you been keeping up your practice?"

"It's only been a few days."

"So no, then." The corners of Ms. W's mouth went down.

"I did do a tweak to make sure you woke up." She didn't want to mention the other part of her wish, unsure if it would seem selfish. She looked again at the nurse—what was she was making of these odd conversations? But she just kept on with her knitting. Could she be deaf?

"Thank you for that." Ms. W shifted, appearing uncomfortable, and the nurse immediately stood to steady her and rearrange pillows. She must be in even worse shape than she looked. "I wanted your impressions from the dinner and from the conversation before. I have the facts from the detective who was just here, but your impressions? Did anyone seem tense or angry? Say anything that seemed strange?"

"Not that I noticed."

"I don't know why any of them should have any animosity toward me." Ms. W's voice shook with distress. "The ones who were close enough to do it, I've been nothing but good to any of them. The detective was too far away. I suppose your little friend could do it with tricks she learned from Simon, but I don't think she has any motive."

It hadn't been phrased as a question, but it was accompanied with a mildly inquisitive look. Marissa answered a little more sharply than she'd intended. "Ruby? Of course not! She's a crusader for justice. She doesn't go around trying to kill people."

Ms. W shrugged. "You know about her past, I take it. And she did do violence to that Sasquatch."

"He was trying to hurt her! I know enough about her past to know she hasn't poisoned anyone."

"Someone did it. I've known all the others for years."

"Just stop it. It wasn't her." She felt tempted to bring up Olga's record which must be far worse than Ruby's, but she felt sure it wasn't her either, so why stir the pot?

There was a knock at the door, and it swung open without waiting for an answer, Olga coming in with a tray balanced on one hand. "Derek said you wanted tea?"

Ms. W gestured to her lap table. "Over here, please."

Olga rounded the bed to the side nearest the little table, leaned over, and set the tray down on the lap table. Ms. W gave her a sharp look and motioned her to come closer. Marissa scooted back to give her access.

"You have a smudge." Ms. W licked her thumb and reached up to rub it over Olga's forehead.

A lot of things seemed to happen at once. Ms. W and Olga each gave a little soft cry, and Olga slumped over the bed, bumping the table and sending the teapot tumbling off the other end. Marissa jumped up and grabbed her, afraid she would hurt Ms. W by falling on her. The ever-alert Maureen also jumped up, grabbing the hot pot before it could hit the floor, then swore and dropped it.

Olga was already beginning to come around, and Marissa steered her to the chair. Ms. W sat up, shedding pillows, and pointed a trembling finger at Olga. "Her! Her! She's the one!"

Wait, what? Was she saying Olga had poisoned her? Olga must be thinking the same thing because she shook her head. "I didn't do it! What'd you do to me, old woman?"

And then Marissa understood. Olga wasn't "the one," she was "The One," with capital letters. Ms. W had touched Olga's forehead, just as she used to do when she was searching, before she'd found what she sought in Marissa—or so she'd thought. Like everyone who'd received that touch, Olga had felt dizzy and disoriented. But unlike everyone, Ms. W was confidently pointing to her. "You have the gift in full measure. I can feel it!"

"What the hell are you talking about?"

Marissa put a hand on her shoulder. "You're the new trainee tweaker." She felt laughter bubbling up and suppressed it. She'd tried to arrange to get Ms. W her protégé back. And it had actually worked! For the second time, her tweak had succeeded—halfway. Ms. W had her protégé, it just wasn't her anymore.

It was actually a relief. At least now she didn't need to decide between that and going to space. And she'd never need to come back here. "Congratulations. I'm sure you'll be better at it than me. You could hardly be worse." She turned to Ms. W. "And I promise you Ruby isn't the poisoner. If I were you, I'd take a look at your nephew. I'm sure he doesn't like the way you boss him around. If there's nothing else, I'll go now." Not waiting for an answer, she left the room, hurried down the stairs, back to the conservatory for what was probably the last time, and out the French doors into the garden, wanting its calming influence.

Not that there was any reason to be upset or anything. This was a good thing, right?

There had been a little rain while she was inside, and the air was cool. She walked on the gravel path, which was dark with water, between the precise topiary creatures, past flower beds with angular patterns of different colors, pausing to watch a bee getting busy with a rose. She took a deep breath of the delicate scent.

Of course, she would miss some of the people in the house. Ithikate and the Goloopa could hardly come out to visit. And it had been cool to be part of something big and secret.

The path meandered past the gnome dome. And Marissa paused, shocked. There was a big triangular chunk knocked out of the dome, cracks radiating out from the exposed red clay edge. A sledgehammer lay on the ground beside it. Who would do such a thing? She ran up to it, and then she saw the other thing. On the wet gravel path, looking comically like a stereotypical chalk outline from some police show, was the silhouette of a human form in lighter, dry gravel. Someone had lain here, their body shielding part of the path from the rain. And now they were gone. But had they left under their own power? It looked like there were drag marks in the gravel leading toward the broken dome.

And then the wind picked up, scattering droplets onto her from a nearby willow tree, and the rain started again, hard, blurring the gruesome outline.

Marissa ran for the front gate, stabbed blindly at the buttons, and once outside, leaned with her palms against the wall, breathing hard and gulping back sobs. A bicycle messenger rode past, ringing his bell, and she moved aside to let him past. She would just go now. She would just go and not come back.

On the bus, headed downtown, her phone pinged with a text. It was from Margo, but she recognized Ms. W's style. *We've learned that Rex Edmunds, the gentleman who visited the house the other day and later trespassed on the grounds, is a freelance journalist. He's been asking questions about us around the neighborhood, and we believe the drones are his, as well. If you meet him, do not give him any information or let him in again.*

Marissa put her phone away without answering. She suspected Mr. Edmunds would no longer be a problem.

But no. He might still be alive underground in the gnome den, somewhere. They needed to know, if she could figure out a way to tell them without telling any eavesdroppers.

She took out the phone.

Simon looked around the card table at the other players in his study. Nominally, they were playing Hearts, but he suspected most, like him, were only half paying attention to the game.

Dr. Sin glanced at his watch. "Late again. What is with these people?" He glared at the desk phone.

The Sasquatch thumbed through his cards. They looked small in his thick fingers. He carefully pulled one out and tossed it down—five of spades.

"I got nothing." Salali threw down a useless nine of clubs. She was the only one of them who seemed focused on the game—but then, this was just a job for her. She'd get paid either way.

The phone rang. Simon started, then stood up quickly and stabbed the "Record" button and the speaker button on the phone.

"Goodnight."

"Do you have the money?" The electronically disguised voice rang out in the suddenly quiet room.

Simon glanced at the backpack on the couch. Three million dollars in hundreds wasn't as large as one might think but had been harder and more expensive to pull together on short notice than he'd hoped. "We've got it."

"That's wise of you. Here are your instructions. In thirty seconds, a small red pickup will pause outside your house. You'll throw my money into the back."

"Fuck," Salali muttered.

"I assume you're smart enough not to have put in any radio trackers or other tricks. Rest assured we'll find them, and the results won't be pretty."

"Delay them," Dr. Sin whispered. "The radio collar isn't here yet."

"Just a minute," Simon said into the phone. "Hello?" He stared at the handset, then sighed and set it down.

Dr. Sin stood. "I'll carry it out." He looked at the mantel where Retractable Blade sat. "Are you game, sir?"

The Skohlar shucked his vest and reached up to remove his earring. Dr. Sin grabbed the handles of the duffel and paused to let Retractable Blade jump onto him, little claws digging into the back of his gray linen suit. Simon went ahead to open the door, glancing at his watch.

The pickup pulled up with a screech, passing the house to stop in front of the Sasquatch's urban assault vehicle. The truck windows were tinted, the driver just a dark blob. Dr. Sin held the bag in front of himself with both hands, staggered to the back of the pickup, and heaved the duffel over the tailgate. As soon as the bag thumped into the truck bed, the vehicle zoomed off.

With a Skohlar on the rear bumper, clinging to the empty license plate frame.

Salali had come out on the steps to watch. As the truck rounded the corner, brakes screeching, she grunted. "How will the rat get in touch once they stop?"

Simon motioned them inside. "I guess he'll get word back however he can. We can't hope to scramble fast enough to catch up to them, but perhaps we'll get a description of the kidnappers." He closed the door behind them. "Once we know who it is, the Guardians can deal with them."

"You're not concerned the bad guys might see him and, like, smell a rat?"

Simon shrugged. "The Skohlars still aren't known to most of The Scene. Even if they see him, I'm hoping they'll just think he's a regular rat. There are plenty of those around, too."

Ruby met Kirk and Marissa at the corner, and they walked to Ujo's studio together. She punched in the door code and followed the others in. Something was clearly bugging Marissa, but she didn't want to ask while Kirk could hear. At the top of the stairs, they split up—they to the left and Kirk to the right. Once they were in the girls' changing room, Ruby asked softly, "Is something wrong?"

"I can't talk about it. I think someone's dead, and I think I'm sorta responsible for it."

"That seems unlikely."

Marissa dumped out a shopping bag onto a bench, ripping into the plastic wrapper of a new Tae Kwan Do uniform. "You don't know. All this weird shit I've been doing. You really don't know."

"I know you don't go around killing people." Ruby pulled her own rolled-up uniform from her backpack.

"I can't talk about it yet." Marissa pulled off her black t-shirt—underneath it she wore a sports bra. "I mean, look, I was the one who lured him onto the property with my croquet ball. If the redcaps ate him, doesn't that make me partly responsible?"

"I'm a little confused. Maybe you could back up, like, three steps."

"I did tell you about this, like, a week ago."

The recent pace of events made a week ago seem like forever, but the croquet ball did sound familiar. "Ms. W gave you a problem to solve. And you solved it, as I recall."

"That's debatable. I mean, yes, someone else's mail did end up in her house, but I don't know whether delivered is the right word, and there were… side effects."

"Start from the top. Here, sit."

Midway through the telling there was a knock on the door. "Are you two almost ready?"

Ruby turned her head. "Go on and start getting beat up without us, Kirk. We'll be just a minute."

A minute later, the tale concluded, Marissa said, "…so I just feel like it's my fault."

"Your fault that a reporter chose to climb over the wall—how did he get past the razor wire?—chose to attack the gnome home with a hammer, and maybe got himself killed?"

"He wouldn't have been there except for me."

"Really? A reporter just happens to move in to the carriage house next door. Then he finds a croquet ball and doesn't just throw it back over the wall like a normal person would. No, he has to return it in person. And not just hand it over to the first person he sees but use it as an excuse to get into the house and talk to people. And then he leaves his mail behind, which to me looks like an excuse to come back and visit some more."

Marissa bit her lip. "You think he was there to find out about Ms. W all along."

"What do you think?"

"When you put it that way, yes, I guess so. But it's so awful what happened."

"It's tragic for him, but the key point here is, it's not one bit your fault. He would've found his way in somehow."

They sat quiet for a while. Dimly, through the wall, came a thud of someone being thrown to the mats. Marissa stood and paced. "It's still horrible. I don't know how you do it."

"Do what, exactly?"

"All this weird stuff. It just doesn't faze you. I mean, look, someone was poisoned, someone's been kidnapped and might die, someone else probably is dead—doesn't it bother you?"

"I… guess it hadn't occurred to me that it should. It's an adventure."

"It bothers me a lot. It's just as well I'm not the Chosen One anymore. I'm feeling more and more I'm not cut out for this weird stuff."

"Wait, what?" Ruby grabbed at her sleeve as she passed. "What do you mean, you're not the Chosen One?"

"Oh, yeah, I forgot that part. Look, I'll tell you and Kirk all about it later. Right now I don't want to be any later for the lesson."

They went in, and Ujo lined them up, had them assume the stance, and gave them a critical look. He wandered down the line, nudged a foot into position with his own foot, adjusted the position of an arm. "Could be worse. Could also be better. Ready? Let's see if you practiced. Eppy! Peppy! Khaki! Hillo! Hollo! Hello!"

When they left, Ruby waited for the others to start down the stairs first. Marissa and Kirk looked as tired and bruised as she felt. Marissa grabbed the front seat in Kirk's car, then twisted to talk to Ruby. "Time to spill. What's the secret project with the Skohlars?"

"How'd you know it was... well, never mind. I'm part of a crack negotiating team. I'm not doing any of the actual negotiating, I'm more a mascot the Skohlars demanded. It's going pretty well, though there's some controversy over my methods."

"When isn't there?" Kirk paused at an intersection to let a woman with a crowd of kids cross the street. "By the way, where are we going?"

Marissa looked up from her phone. "I've got some time. It's been a while since we all got together. Can we go to Revenge for a talk and maybe some lunch?"

"I'm game," Ruby said. "Anyway, the Skohlars. I think they trust me a little because they like my name. They kinda prefer names that mean something."

"Most names *do* mean something, if you think about it," Marissa said. "Just not in English. If you had as many pregnant older cousins as I have, you'd know that. My name means 'of the sea.' In Latin or Greek or something."

Kirk glanced at her. "What about my name?"

"Hang on, I'll look it up." She took out her phone. "Baby names website, here I come."

Ruby checked her own phone for texts and emails that might have arrived during the lesson while it was turned off.

"Kirk means a church. Not fitting in your case since I don't believe you ever visit one, but how could your parents know that when they named you? Ruby, is there any news about Spider?"

"No, but they wouldn't necessarily tell me anyway, especially on what Simon calls the 'official government listening device.' Even with the encryption app."

"He has a point," Kirk said. "Especially while the investigation about Ms. W is still going on. What's the latest news? Marissa?"

"Nothing from the police, but Olga has a theory. She emailed me."

Kirk slowed as he approached a corner. "Right or left here?"

"Left." Ruby leaned forward between the seats. "What is this theory?"

"She thinks someone was planning something, and when Ms. W started giving out presents, they figured she was doing a tweak to stop them, so they panicked and tried to kill her."

"Planning something like a kidnapping? But Olga doesn't know about the kidnapping, does she? You didn't tell her."

"No, but maybe *we* know enough to put some things together."

"Wait, though." Kirk stopped at a red light and looked at them over his shoulder. "I thought Ms. W couldn't predict things. She wouldn't know there'd be a kidnapping beforehand."

Marissa nodded. "Yah. So it couldn't have been about the kidnapping, but maybe they thought it was."

"Um," Ruby said.

"Okay, she knows something." Marissa pointed at Ruby's nose. "Spill it."

"Go, the light is green. Yeah, I do know something. I overheard Karomeenut talking with Simon—"

"And Karomeenut is…?"

"One of the head Sasquatches. He said he told Ms. W about Spider's job in advance and asked her to make sure nothing went wrong."

Marissa grunted. "Maybe that's what the dinner was about, then. She gave everyone those gifts to try to avoid potential problems."

Kirk pulled up in front of the coffeeshop and turned off the car. "It doesn't seem to have worked."

Marissa thought. "Well no, but the request was a little vague. It would be hard to come up with a tweak that would cover every possibility of something going wrong. Could be why there were so many people and so many gifts at the dinner."

Kirk jingled his keys and shoved them into his pocket. "Okay, that doesn't really tell us who did it, though, does it? I guess we'll just have to hope Ms. W wakes up and can just tell us what was going on. Let's go have coffee!"

"Oh, that was the other thing." Marissa put a hand on his forearm to keep him in the car. "She is awake, but she doesn't remember what the grand tweak was about."

"Brain damage?" Ruby asked.

"It might come back to her with time or if someone asks her specifically about Sasquatches. But it'll have to be someone else—I'm not going back there."

Ruby sat back to listen to Marissa tell the whole story of her day—the bits she'd heard already and the bits that were new to her.

"That's awful. I mean, about that reporter." Kirk reached out as if to put his hand on Marissa's but put it back on the steering wheel. "You must hate the idea of going back there."

"Yes, thank you. I'm glad someone gets it. Not that I have any reason to go there anymore, so it's just as well." Marissa shouldered her backpack and opened the car door. "I wonder whether they have any of those turkey wraps today."

Ruby thought of something else while they were waiting in line but couldn't talk about it until they were at their usual secluded corner booth with their food. It was their usual table precisely because of the seclusion, since their conversation often involved things mundanes shouldn't overhear. She leaned forward and lowered her voice. "If she was poisoned to keep her from stopping the kidnapping, the kidnapper must've been at the dinner. But the people who live there have barely left the house, and the police must be watching them closely anyway. They couldn't be going off and feeding prisoners."

"No," Marissa said. "But they could actually be working with the kidnappers."

Kirk unwrapped his sandwich. "The amount of money that's involved, it could be any of them. Too bad we can't listen in on the ransom calls. Maybe we could figure out who."

"Oh, but we can. Listen, I mean. I've got the recordings here." Marissa unzipped her pack. "Not from today, if there was one today, but the first two."

Ruby rolled her eyes. "If Simon knew you were carrying those around town, he'd freak."

"Cool your jets, girl. I know how to make a computer secure." She set her little laptop on the table. It was the same one she'd had since Ruby had known her, but she'd covered it with so many decals of skulls, lightning bolts, and nebulas, that little of the original pink color was visible. She took out a lightweight wireless headset and handed it to Kirk. "Here's the first one."

She played both calls and explained her theory about Spider's coded message. "But I must've gotten it wrong, though, because they weren't where I thought."

"But they only tried one place?" Kirk spoke around a bite of sandwich. "I mean, there are a bunch of recycling places in town. There could be more than one with a vacant lot and a view of downtown."

Marissa's hands paused for a moment over the keyboard. She looked up. "Recycling?"

"Yeah, my dad collects metal to sell, and he takes it to Sal's Recycling. I think that's what they mostly call themselves."

"I only searched for scrap metal." She started typing. "Okay, there are a bunch more places with recycling in the name. Shit! It'll take a while to see which of these are near vacant lots."

"Actually…." Ruby leaned in to look at the screen. "Are any of them just south of a lot of train tracks? Because he said he was under considerable strain, and that's…"

"An anagram for trains. Gotcha." She reached for the mouse.

"Why did he mention the Prudential building specifically?" Kirk moved in so he could see the screen too. "If he can see it, he must also be able to see some others that are bigger."

"I thought maybe the place was on the same street, but I didn't see any." She switched to satellite view and zoomed in. "But here's one. And look, there's an empty lot just across the street." She switched to street view. "And an empty-looking building with a tiny window on the second floor that can probably see all three things." She looked at the others. "I think this is it."

"Great. I'm calling Simon." Ruby let it ring until she got a voice mail greeting. "Hey Unc. They might be at this address." She read it from the screen. "Let me know you got this."

"No answer?"

Ruby started composing a text message. "They're probably doing the radio silence thing while they track the kidnapper. Who am I kidding, he never answers my calls anyway." She dictated a text message. *Listen to your voice mail. Important.* And then she tried Dr. Sin. She didn't have Karomeenut's number but scrolled back through her call history to find the number of another Elder. No answer. She sat on the couch next to Marissa, staring at the screen.

Marissa shut the cover of her computer. "I can tell what you're thinking, and you are not doing that."

"Who knows how long before he gets it? Someone should go over there now and free them."

"Not you, though. We'll call Captain Urbana."

"But what if we're wrong? They specifically said to keep her out of it. If we spill the beans for nothing and she stops them from paying the ransom…."

Kirk had actually stopped eating to participate in the conversation. "But they said on the call that was supposed to happen this morning."

"Yeah, but what if it didn't? What if it got delayed? Nobody tells me anything."

"This is not something *you* need to do." Marissa put the computer away. "Tell Urbana to take a few of her folks and search the place. Just don't say why."

"Yeah, she totally trusts me, so she'll do that if I just ask."

"Call Derek then."

"That's a…" Actually, Derek just might go along with it. "… pretty good idea." She looked back through her photos—way back, to find the one she'd taken of his business card when they'd first met, when he was investigating Simon. She punched in the number, and it rang twice.

"*Yah?*"

"Hey, it's Ruby. Listen, I got a clue in the… in the Ms. Wheelwright case." Who knows, that might even be true. "Can you meet us at this address, please?"

Marissa hissed, "Really, really stupid!"

Ruby waved her down and repeated it from memory. "It's a salvage business. Pretend you're shopping and keep an eye on the empty warehouse across the street. We'll be there as soon as we can."

Kirk had resumed eating. "So." He swallowed. "He probably assumed by 'we' you meant you and some adults."

"I can't help what he assumes." She stood. "Are you two coming?"

Kirk wrapped the rest of his sandwich in its plastic. "I'm in."

Marissa threw up her hands. "You're crazy!"

"Come on, M. It's not like we're going into battle. We just need to know if they're really there. If we see Spider waving to us from that window, we'll know it's okay to call in the big guns."

Kirk stood, picking up his gym bag. "Yeah, you should come. It'll be an adventure."

Marissa also stood, hefting her backpack over one shoulder. She looked at Kirk, biting her lip.

He looked back, narrow-eyed. "What?"

She counted off on her fingers. "One, I've had enough adventure for one day. Two, it's too soon for us to make an album. Three, there's nothing wrong with pink. I like pink. I don't really care for black."

"What does that have to do with—"

"I like the hair, though. I'll keep the hair." She threaded her other arm through the backpack strap. "You two have fun. If you get killed, I'll write you a nice eulogy."

Kirk watched her walk away. "I'm not sure what just happened."

Ruby grabbed his sleeve and pulled toward the door. "Later. We've gotta go."

"How sure are we this is the right place?"

Ruby got out of the car and leaned on the roof to look, then pulled back because it was broiling hot. "Ow. Who knows?" The building across the vacant lot was sooty red brick with a crack running up the side. The side facing downtown was mostly blank, with just two tiny windows high up. If Spider could look out of those, he probably could see his four clues, including the rail yard over the roof of the low building they'd stopped in front of. "Let's find Derek. Maybe he's seen something."

The detective was in the scrap yard with a little muscular man in striped coveralls leaning over the engine of some old car. She saw him glance across the street through the tall chain link fence, then he spotted them and waved. "If that looks okay after you get it off, I'll take it," he told the other man. He looked past Ruby and Kirk as he approached, wiping his hands on a paper napkin. He led them around a corner out of sight of the scrapyard owner but still with a view of the target building. "Where's everyone else?"

"This is everyone for now. Any activity across the street?"

"All quiet. What do you mean this is everyone? Never mind, I guess I should know better by now. It's you, after all. You did have a larger *squad* of kids last time, though, at least."

"Too short notice to round up the gang. A bunch of Sasquatches were kidnapped, and we think they're being held here. They could be in danger. Also, the kidnapper could come back, and we don't want them to get away."

"Kidnapping?" Derek stuffed the napkin in his pocket. "What have you gotten yourselves into this time, and what does it have to do with Ms. Wheelwright?"

"That's just a guess," Kirk said. "But even if we're wrong about that, we still need to rescue the Sasquatches."

"And why did you call me instead of Captain Urbana? Where's your uncle?"

Kirk looked at Ruby. Ruby looked at Kirk. "We, uh, tried calling several people, but you were the only one who answered. As long as we're here, we should check whether this is the right place before we bother anyone else, don't you think?"

At that moment, Ruby's phone rang, and she snatched it out of her pocket, almost dropping it in her haste to answer. "Hey, Unc. What's poppin'?"

"I just got your message. What's going on? Where are you?"

"We're across the street from the suspected kidnapper hideout, just chilling and keeping an eye on the place."

"Didn't we just talk about not going into dangerous situations without backup?"

"We have backup—Detective Derek is here. And we're not going in, like I said, just watching."

"Keep doing that. We should be there in twenty-eight minutes. What have you seen?"

Derek held out his hand for the phone. "Is that Simon? I've been

IFO fifteen minutes with no activity. The kids just got here and haven't said much, so please explain." He paused, listening. "Yeah. Yeah. North side, solid looking metal door, padlocked. I didn't walk around the other sides, but it's the kind of place I'd expect a loading dock around back." He pointed at Kirk. "Hey, kid. Kirk, right? Wanna run around the block and see whether there's other doors or any signs of life?"

"I'll go," Ruby said.

The phone made a squawk. "Your uncle says not," Derek reported unnecessarily. "In any case, it sounds like this is an inside job, so if someone sees you walking past, they might recognize you, but they won't know him, right? Go on, boy, and try to look casual. If you want to look natural, keep your eyes on your phone."

Kirk went, and while Ruby fumed, Derek continued using her phone. "Okay, keep talking. Yeah. Yeah. Fuck. All right, I'll call back if anything changes." He hung up.

Ruby grabbed the phone from his hand. "Talk. What happened?"

"They delivered the ransom per instructions, except they planted a Skohlar on the getaway vehicle. They hadn't had time to arrange a way for him to communicate back, so it was a while before they heard back. Their, uh, guy managed to follow the package for a while, then he was spotted, and they threw something at him, so he took off. But he overheard them mention an address. So Simon and some folks went to check it out, but it was a dud."

"You think the kidnapper gave a wrong address on purpose to fool them?"

Derek nodded. "While they were coming back from there, they got another call from the kidnapper, who accused them of breaking the deal and said they were going to kill the hostages."

"What? Well, we have to stop them!"

"We've got nothing to stop them with, assuming they're even here."

"You have a gun!"

"Actually, at the moment, I don't. My carry permission was suspended because I couldn't explain why I'd discharged ten rounds on a certain night you may recall."

"Oh. Sorry." The first of the rounds in question had been fired at Kirk, fortunately missing, and the rest, equally ineffective, were aimed at the certain death that was trying to catch Kirk in its slavering jaws. "But we have to do something."

"We wait for backup. Charging in unarmed on violent criminals is just a good way to get killed. They might not even be here."

Ruby's phone pinged with a text from Kirk. *Loading dock dark red Nissan Sentra.* A photo followed, displaying the car with license plate visible parked with its nose against a brick wall.

Derek leaned over to look at her screen. "That might not mean anything. People will park anywhere that's free."

"There's plenty of free parking on this street, though. And I've seen this car recently—or one just like it, at least. It was in Ms. W's driveway when I went to her dinner. Who does it belong to? Spider rides a motorcycle."

"Anyone living there has their own garage spaces. And I saw Doctor Sin arrive by cab."

They looked at each other for a moment.

"That leaves only Netta Polacek," Ruby said.

"Would she recognize a Skohlar?"

"Her husband was working for them when he died."

"Does she have anything against Sasquatches?"

"Well… one of them did release the monster that killed him."

"Right. You wait here. Let the others know about this. Do not move. Got it?"

Ruby hefted her phone. "Only my thumbs will move."

"Perfect." Derek hurried out the gate.

The junkyard owner showed up, a filthy engine part dangling from one hand, watching him leave. "Hey, he's taking off without the part he wanted."

"He'll be back. Meanwhile, I don't suppose you have anything here like a weapon?"

The man scratched his bald head. "I don't carry guns."

"Sure, but like a sword or a mace maybe."

"What's a mace? You mean the spray?"

"No, like a baseball bat with spikes."

"What kind of place do you think this is? I've got a pile of old rebar over there, but the way you're asking for it, I don't know if I should let you have any."

"Relax, the guy we're with is a policeman." As she went over to examine the pile, Ruby rapidly sent a couple of texts. Then she looked at the time. Twenty-three minutes before they could expect the cavalry. How long did it take to kill a few Sasquatches? She knew from experience they weren't easy to take down. Her own notions ran to explosives, but Netta—if it really was her—would probably want something quieter.

The gate clanged, and Kirk hurried up to her, breathing hard. "Where's the detective?"

"I don't know. He said to wait here." The rebar was mostly a twisted, rusty mess with chunks of concrete still sticking to it, but there were a few long, straight pieces that looked like they might not be too heavy for her. "Choose a weapon. It might be close quarters in there, so I'm thinking something with a point in case there's not room to swing."

"We're not going in there, though."

"The kidnapper called Simon and said they were going to kill the Sasquatches. I don't think we can afford to wait—" she looked at her phone "—twenty-two minutes." She bent and took up a thin, rusty bar about the length of her practice sword. Heavy, but manageable, if only it had a better grip. "Find yourself something. I'll see if that guy has duct tape or something to make a handle."

There was duct tape in plenty, and Ruby was able to convince the proprietor to part with two rolls with the promise that Derek would pay for them. As she walked away, unrolling a length and wrapping it around the end of the rod, the walking piggy bank in question returned, carrying a tire iron in one hand and something that looked like a beat-up model of the starship Enterprise in the other.

Derek looked at her improvised weapon. "What are you doing?"

"Preparing to rescue some hostages. If it's just Netta, we can take her. She's small, and I'll make her afraid. You owe that guy twenty dollars by the way."

"We're not going in there, and we know for a fact she's not working alone." He hefted the starship. "For now I'll just make sure she can't drive off with the ransom. She won't be able to escape me on foot."

"I care a great deal more about saving the Sasquatches than some old ransom money, and so do the other Sasquatches. But if we hurry we can save them both."

"Sasquatches?" The junkyard guy had come walking up while they were talking.

Derek turned to him, scowling. "Yeah, you know. The baseball team. Minor league."

"What's this about ransoms?"

Derek tucked the tire iron under his arm, reached into his inside suit pocket, and flashed his badge. "Police business. Seriously now, back off."

"Why are these kids arming themselves? You're not taking them to fight bad guys."

"Of course not. In fact, you'll watch them for me while I deal with this. Don't let them leave until this is over." He shook his tire iron at her. "Stay. Got it?"

Ruby continued wrapping the handle of her impromptu rapier. "Got it. Better hurry. She might drive off any second."

He looked at the sky like one seeking answers from above, shook his head, and ran for the gate. Kirk walked over, experimentally swinging a thick metal rod. "What's the plan?"

She handed him the other roll of tape. "We wait one minute, then follow. Hurry up and make yourself a handle."

"I *have* a handle. Fnar, fnar."

"Young lady—"

Ruby rounded on the junkyard man, brandishing her weapon. "You don't have the right to keep us here just because a policeman asks you to. We're not under arrest, so we're free to leave. Plus we're armed, so you just keep your distance. Kirk, hurry up."

"You can't leave without paying for that stuff, though."

"Dammit! Kirk, do you have twenty bucks? Good. Just drop it and let's go. Not the rebar, dummy. Drop the money." She kept the pointy end of her rod between herself and the junk man as she half-backed up to the gate, then they were out on the street, Kirk still building up layers of tape for his handle as they hurried across. "I don't understand. He's not going in, is he? Aren't we supposed to wait for Simon and them? It looked like he's just going to boot that car."

"Oh, is that what that thing was?" Thinking back on it, the starship thing had been about the right size to clamp around a car tire. "I think he'll need help guarding the exit. Were there any other doors besides the ones at the loading dock?"

"One, but it was padlocked from the outside, so I don't think they'll leave that way."

"Great. Then we'll just help Derek guard the exit until the others show up." Or until she could convince him to enter.

As they rounded the corner of the building, they heard running footsteps behind them. Ruby turned, heart pounding, brandishing her weapon, and Kirk raised his over his shoulder in a two-handed grip. It was the junk guy, running after them, holding a ginormous knife in a leather sheath.

"You can't stop us," Kirk said.

Junk guy halted. "No, I see that. So I thought I'd help. Keep you from getting yourselfs killed."

Ruby looked at Kirk who looked at Ruby. She shrugged. "Fine. Come on, then. What's your name?"

"I'm Earl." He fell into step beside them. "What's happened? Someone kidnapped a whole ball team?"

Kirk glanced at him. "Ball team? What—I mean, no, just a few, um, players."

They rounded the corner of the building, and Ruby saw the red car. Derek crouched beside it, trying to close the latch on his car boot while keeping watch on the dock doors—one normal sized metal one and two giant garage style loading doors. He must've heard them approaching because he scrambled to his feet, clutching up his tire iron from the crumbling asphalt. "Oh, it's you. Should've known. Are you completely incapable of following instructions?"

Ruby shrugged. "Pretty much."

He knelt to close the clamp with a definitive clack. "Got yourself another minion besides, I see. Not sure how you do it."

"I didn't try to convince him to help. Sometimes the minions, they just… accumulate."

"Well, no one's leaving now, so you and your accumulation can just back off."

"I'm a mite unclear on what's going on," Earl said. "Might those people harm the ball players? They don't know the cops have found 'em, right?"

"It's a delicate situation." Derek motioned them against the wall, out of view for anyone who might look out the narrow barred upper-floor windows. "When the others arrive, they should have concussion grenades?" The question was directed at Ruby.

She thought back to when she'd seen them suiting up. Their bodies had been hung with various pouches and holsters, but they hadn't paused to give her an inventory. "Um, possibly? Beanbag guns for sure. Did you call Captain Urbana?"

"Yes, but her people can't get here soon enough."

Earl looked at one and the other of them with confusion. "Why are you asking this girl what the cops are packing? *You're* the cop, I thought."

Derek frowned. "This is some, uh, private security hired by the, you know, the ball team."

From inside the building, there came a long, angry animal howl followed by booming sounds. Earl ducked, then looked at the big loading dock doors in wonder. "What was *that?*"

Ruby grabbed Derek's sleeve. "She's doing it. She threatened to kill them, and she's doing it right now."

Derek glanced at his watch.

"Twelve minutes," Kirk announced. "Too long."

Derek huffed and glared at the sky. "Fine. Kirk, switch weapons with me." Testing the balance of the rebar sword, he turned to Earl. "You're with me if you're willing. You two, *wait here,* dammit."

Earl looked nervously at the building, then took a firmer grip on his knife and hurried up the half-flight of stairs after the detective. Derek grabbed the handle of the service door and tugged, but it wouldn't budge. "Locked," he muttered.

Kirk stepped back to look up. "I don't suppose knocking would be a good idea."

"Hey," Ruby said. "Ms. W gave you lock picks. Do you have them?"

"I do, but I don't know how to use them."

"Um," Earl said, raising his hand. "I, uh, sorta do."

Derek patted his pockets and came out with the slim folder. "This one time, I won't ask. Go for it."

"Hurry," Ruby urged.

Another howl and a series of thumps came from inside, and Earl fumbled, dropping a pick and then catching it in midair. He leaned in, closing his eyes, and after twenty seconds of fiddling, the lock clicked. Derek had descended two steps to give him room to work, but when the door opened, he pushed past into the dark interior, Earl close at his heels.

After a few seconds, there was a shout—Derek, probably—and a high shriek and a crash. The Sasquatches howled again, two at once this time, and kept beating on whatever they were beating on.

"Now?" Kirk asked.

"Now." Ruby ran up the stairs, weapon at the ready. After the bright outdoors, she couldn't see what was going on, but she could hear a scuffle up ahead. Someone grunted, and there was another crash, and by then her eyes had adjusted enough to see Derek fighting a couple of chonky black... well she wasn't sure what they were, but she would bet whoever created the Michelin Man logo had seen one. They were roughly human-shaped but made of stacks of thick disks, flailing at the detective with heavy block-shaped fists. Earl was on the floor, crawling toward the door, while Derek swung his weapon, clanging against the walls of the narrow hallway and failing to get up enough speed to do much damage. One of the creatures grabbed his wrist, stopping him.

Ruby lunged forward, pointing her rebar rapier, and pushed the point into the gap between Derek and the wall to punch the Michelin Man right in the... middle tube.

The creature gave a plaintive whistle and fell, releasing Derek to clutch at itself. Derek planted a foot on the thing's leg and took advantage of the opening to make an overhead swing, bringing the heavy bar down with a solid thud on the other creature's head. It fell back without a sound, and Derek gave the one that was already down and struggling the same treatment.

Derek turned, and though it was a little too dark to make out his expression, his voice was plenty annoyed. "I told you to stay the hell out."

The howling and pounding from the next room was now going on non-stop, and she had to shout. "Good thing for you I didn't listen. Get a move on!"

Earl had gotten up by this time, and the four of them crowded through the doorway. Kirk, the last through, gave a shout and fell. A squarish black hand had emerged from the doorway and grabbed him by the ankle, hauling him back.

Derek pointed to Earl. "You, help him. Use the knife if you have to, but don't kill it. Ruby, stay here."

The room they were in was large and tall with huge garage-style doors large enough not just to unload semi-trucks, but to actually fit an entire semi-trailer inside. She knew this because someone had actually done so. It was from this heavy-duty trailer that the howling and pounding came. What was getting the creatures so upset? Was someone inside there trying to hurt them? The idea seemed ridiculous. There hadn't been any shots fired, and anyone tangling with a Sasquatch would get pounded to jelly in about a second.

Derek started for the back of the trailer, while Ruby looked around for other threats. The room was fairly well lit with long fluorescents and had catwalks around the edges and cranes and pulleys and things in the ceiling. It might have been used to assemble large machinery to be shipped out the big doors, but the equipment looked old and rusty now. As Derek reached the rear doors of the trailer, someone on top of the trailer stepped up to the edge, staring at Ruby and beyond, wild-eyed.

"Netta!" Ruby shouted. "You're caught! The building is surrounded!" Behind her, there were renewed sounds of struggle in the hallway, which she tried to ignore. "Surrender peacefully!"

The trailer doors were secured with a large padlock, and Derek whaled away at it with his piece of rebar. This got Netta's attention, and she ran to the back, brandishing a huge wrench.

"Derek! Watch out!" There was a metal ladder midway along the trailer, and Ruby ran to it, starting to climb. She couldn't see what was happening in back, but there was a crash and a moan, which might've been a Sasquatch. The trailer shook as she climbed from an impact inside. She pulled herself up the ladder, the bare metal rungs cutting into her fingers, but as she neared the top, Netta appeared above, swinging her damned wrench.

Ruby pulled her hand back just in time, the wrench clanging against the rung she'd been holding. Ruby pointed at Netta, holding on desperately with the other hand. "Speck! Tornado!"

She felt Speck whiz past her cheek, then Netta gave a cry and stumbled back, the wrench falling with a clang. Ruby hurried up the last few rungs. Netta was sitting on her butt, swatting at Speck, but seemed to have realized he was more an annoyance then a real threat. Ruby lunged for the wrench, and Netta reached for her pocket, pulling something out, leaping at Ruby, reaching out to grab her sleeve with one hand while the other stabbed at her.

Ruby tried to pull away but felt something jab into her chest. There was a flat electric snap....

And Netta cried out, fell with a crash, twitching on top of the trailer. A small black and chrome device fell from her hand. The tiny taser Ms. W had given her. It must have been defective, because Ruby had felt barely a tingle, but Netta seemed to be out of the action.

Maybe not for long, though. Ruby picked up the wrench and looked around. What had Netta been doing with it? The top of the trailer had vents and things on it, but one thing that looked out of place was a yellow gas canister with a thick black hose connected to the roof of the trailer. Was it pumping gas into the trailer? Whatever it was, Ruby had better shut it off fast because the howling and pounding from inside was definitely sounding weaker. The hose was secured to the trailer with a big nut—hence the wrench—but it would probably be faster to shut the valve on top of the cylinder. "Righty tighty," she muttered. "Lefty loosey." Hopefully that rule held true in this case. She wanted to shut it off, not open it full blast.

There was a clanging on the ladder, and Kirk's head popped over the edge, He brandished his tire iron. "What's going on? Are you okay?"

"She was gassing them, but I think I've got it shut off. Hold her down, okay?"

Netta seemed to be recovering from the effects of the shock, but

Kirk climbed the rest of the way up and pushed her down, twisting one arm behind her back. "Sorry," he muttered.

"You don't have to be sorry. She was trying to do murder. What's going on down there?"

"The others are trying to get the lock open, I guess." He gave Ruby an admiring look. "You beat her on your own?"

Ruby thought of Ms. W's booby-trapped gift and Speck. "Not *all* on my own."

"Still, nice going."

"Hold her still." Ruby leaned over to pat Netta's jeans pockets. Finding a bulge in one of them, she crammed her hand in and pulled out a keyring. She'd have to ask her later where she'd found women's jeans with actual usable pockets.

"I'll fucking kill you," Netta said.

Okay, maybe they wouldn't be exchanging shopping tips. "We'll see about that." Ruby ran to the back of the trailer and looked down at Derek and Earl, who'd stuck the piece of rebar through the lock hasp and were working together to lever it open. "Hey." Ruby dropped the keys. "Try these."

By the time she got down to the floor and around back, Derek had the lock open and was yanking on a big lever to open the doors. There was no more noise from inside, which was worrisome. "We may want to stand clear. They're probably unconscious. But if not, they'll be mighty angry."

"But we're rescuing them!" Earl said.

Ruby pulled him away. "Better safe than sorry."

The doors swung open.

The first thing she noticed was the smell, rank and sewery and thick as soup. It came pouring out in a wave, and she held her breath to step up beside Derek to look inside.

The prisoners were piled in the back, a huge mound of brown and black fur. She couldn't tell whether they were alive. "Golly," Earl breathed, and Ruby looked around to find he had a cell phone in his hand, lens pointed into the trailer. Derek stretched to grab it from his hand.

"Hey!"

"Sorry, no photos."

"Can I get some help up here?" Kirk shouted. "She's trying to get away, and I don't want to have to break her arm."

Derek stepped away from the opening as Ruby moved past him to check on the Sasquatches. "You wait here," he told Earl, heading for the ladder.

"What about my phone?"

"Be quiet." Ruby leaned in to tentatively touch a hairy neck. "This one has a pulse." She moved to the next, then the next. All five were still alive. "Say, did anyone tell our backup not to charge in, guns blazing?"

Earl shrugged. "I reckon not."

Ruby pulled out her phone and wrote three quick texts to Simon. *Site secured. Victims unconscious. Still hurry.* What happened if the cops stopped a speeding vehicle with a Sasquatch in it? Presumably there was some way to deal with that.

"Okay," Derek shouted from around the corner. "Let her drop!" There was a thud and a grunt.

"Are you okay?" Kirk, from above.

"Mostly." Derek returned, pushing a glaring Netta ahead of him. "Are they alive?"

"For now. A couple are in bad shape. And we need to free Spider." She pointed up at the second floor rooms behind the railing. "He's probably up there."

Derek gave her a hard look. "There's another prisoner? Why am I only hearing about this now? Why wouldn't he be held with these?"

"He was driving the truck. I don't know about you, but if I kidnapped a truckload of Sasquatches, I wouldn't open the door to shove in another prisoner or for any reason. I'd keep it locked. Have you seen how they're built?"

Kirk came around the corner and peered into the trailer. Spotting the twisted padlock on the floor, keys still in it, he scooped them up. "I'll find Spider."

"Not by yourself. Fetch me that chair, will you?" Derek looked at his prisoner and at Earl, clucking his tongue. "You. I didn't get your name."

"Earl."

"Earl, please stay here, guard the prisoner, and protect Ruby and the… ballplayers. What happened to those things in the hallway?"

"When I come at them with my knife, they broke into pieces, and the pieces ran away. Weirdest thing I ever seen." Earl glanced at the Sasquatches. "Even counting these, which don't look like ballplayers to me."

Derek gave a rueful grin. "No, these are Sasquatches. Sorry I couldn't tell you before."

"And those other critters?"

"No clue. But if any pieces come around, chase 'em off." Derek pointed to where he wanted the chair, and Kirk set it down. "Earl, please secure the prisoner." He handed over a few more large white zip-ties like the one that bound Netta's hands.

Earl pushed Netta into the chair, an ancient, sturdy wooden one with a big splash of paint on the seat. He checked her hands and secured each ankle to a chair leg.

Netta watched this procedure impassively. "I don't recognize you. Why are you helping them?"

"Ma'am, the gentleman who just left is a police officer, so I reckon he has the right to arrest you. I'm just helping out."

"He's not going to *arrest* me, you idiot. What would they charge me with? You think they can haul those… *those things* into the courtroom? No, they're just going to disappear me. My little boy will never know what became of me."

Earl frowned at the Sasquatch pile, and Ruby's heart sank. She'd forgotten about Raymond, who'd just lost his dad, who'd been plotting revenge against those he thought responsible, and who now, very likely, would lose his mom too. How would he react? Who would care for him?

Still, Netta had created this situation herself. Ruby turned to Earl. "These are people. When they wake up, you'll see that for yourself. They deserve protection, like anyone else."

"But is it true she's not getting a trial?"

"She'll get a trial. Just not from a regular court. I was on trial that way myself a while back. If she has a legitimate reason for what she did, they're reasonable. But you saw for yourself she was trying to kill these people."

"These creatures killed my husband." Netta leaned to the side to catch Earl's eye. "Hey. Are you going to stand by and allow this vigilante justice?"

Ruby stepped closer to her. "These *people* were in Canada or somewhere and had nothing to do with your husband's death. The one responsible was already punished. Why did you have to do this? You have the insurance money. You could've just walked away."

"Ha! I've got shit. There's no insurance money. Did you forget? Your *little friends* stole Alasdair's body before they could officially identify him, so they're not paying up." Netta's voice shook, and her face had that ugly trying-not-to-cry look.

"Oh. Well, I'm sorry about that. But the Sasquatches felt really bad about the whole mess. If you'd asked them for help—"

"Yeah, right. I can list on the fingers of zero hands the times they've been helpful to my family. Even when Simon was out of town, did they ever hire Alasdair for anything? No, they'd just wait for him to come back, the snooty bastards."

"Maybe they could tell you consider them creatures instead of people. If a human had been responsible for your husband's death, would that give you the right to punish all humans?"

Netta gave her an exasperated look and turned to Earl. "Do these look like people to you?"

"Before you decide," Ruby said, "I should mention that she probably also poisoned an old woman."

Netta snorted. "You can't prove that."

"I read mysteries, and I've noticed only guilty people say you can't prove it. Innocent ones just say they didn't do it. Too bad for you your scheme didn't work. Even unconscious from a stroke, she managed to stop you."

Earl shuffled his feet. "I don't reckon I know enough yet to be sure what's the right here, but I can say I don't much care for your methods of operating, ma'am. I'll just let things fall out as they will for now."

"And I think I hear the others pulling up outside," Ruby said.

Simon and company had beat their time estimate by two minutes, clattering up the metal stairs outside and echoing in the hallway. Karomeenut hurried up to his people with a large black bag, pulling out a green and white cylinder and breathing mask, which he applied to the smaller female, wrinkling his nose at the smell. "What did chee uthe on them? What thort of gath?"

"I don't know. Yellow tank, on the roof. Didn't notice any particular smell from it." At least not on top of everything else.

"Thimon! Bring down the tank!" He glared at Netta, who was being hustled past by Salali. She glared back.

Dr. Sin looked past Karomeenut into the trailer. "Did you encounter anyone besides Mrs. Polacek?"

Earl pointed at the hallway door. "There was some oddball critters as came all apart, and the parts ran off."

"That could be a couple different things."

"I think some parts are still there if you want to see."

"Lead on. Who are you, anyway?"

"I'm Earl. I run the scrap yard across the way. Listen, one of your guys took my phone, and I gotta get it back."

It didn't look like they needed her help with the Sasquatches, so Ruby followed Dr. Sin and Earl. She'd been itching to see these wandering segments, but none had come her way. Earl asked lots of questions, which Dr. Sin ignored.

The hallway was empty of "critter parts," but they found Spider, Kirk, and Derek leaning against a wall of wire-reinforced glass, looking into what seemed to have once been an office. Inside, fat black disks of various sizes scuttled around on little legs.

"I think we caught about three quarters of the pieces." Derek pointed to a couple of smaller disks sitting quietly in the corner. "I'm not sure those bits are still alive. They were, um, the heads, I guess, and I walloped them pretty good. Thought I should put 'em here anyway, to be sure."

Dr. Sin frowned through the glass. "They're Jadderies. Those segments will probably recover in time. They're pretty tough. But since they were caught in a crime, they probably won't reconstitute as the same individuals, so we may not be able to get much information from them. Spider, did these things help capture you?"

"Yeah, man. They must've been following me. They jumped me when I was locking up the trailer at Escanaba River. They were working with a human woman, but she wore a mask and had a voice gadget. Did you catch her?"

Sin nodded. "Netta Polacek."

"Yeah, thought it might be her. She had a familiar walk. But I don't know how she knew what I was doing and where to find me."

"Hey guys, look," Earl said. "You gotta give me my phone back so I can get the pitchers I took. And I want pitchers of these things, too. This is a free country. I got a right."

"That's true." Dr. Sin looked at Derek. "How long ago did you meet this gentleman?"

Derek looked at his watch. "Oh, forty-five minutes? Less than an hour."

"What difference does that make?" Earl asked, but Dr. Sin was busy with a pocket of his tactical vest. He pulled out a little plastic envelope and flipped through the contents.

Spider tapped Earl's shoulder. "Hey, man, check this out." He pointed to something in the office.

"What are we lookin' at?"

"Fifteen, thirty, here we go." Dr. Sin took out a paper wrapper, like a bandage envelope, ripped it open, and in one smooth motion slapped it against the side of Earl's neck.

"What the hell, man?" Earl stumbled back, raising his hand. "What'd you put on me?" He tried to peel it off, a blue disk about two inches across, but his fingers couldn't get any purchase, and a few seconds later his eyes glazed over, and he slumped.

Dr. Sin caught him and eased him to the floor. "I don't like to do that, but it's only an hour, so he'll probably just think he dozed off. He won't remember any of you."

"That's really unfair!" Ruby put her hands on her hips. "He was really helpful and brave. He should get to remember."

"It does seem pretty egregious," Kirk said.

Dr. Sin grimaced. "When they insist on taking pictures, they're always going to be a problem. We couldn't have trusted him. His business is just across the street, he said?"

"It's the salvage place, yeah." Derek leaned over Earl and pried up an eyelid. "He's really out. That's strong stuff. It really works?"

Dr. Sin raised an eyebrow. "I've used it on you before. You tell me."

"What? Really?"

"Maybe. The point is you can't tell. Do you think we can get him back over there without anyone noticing? The street seems quiet."

Derek gave Dr. Sin a hard look. "Don't mess with my head. The gate's big enough to drive in, so I suppose we could put him on the back seat of my car and get him in without anyone seeing. He does have a security camera, though."

"We can fix that. I don't suppose he's an alcoholic? We could splash a little gin on him."

"That's mean," Ruby said. "What if he's a *recovering* alcoholic, what'll he think happened?"

"Fine, fine. Simple nap it is, then. Let's go, we only have about twenty minutes before he wakes up."

Ruby explored the building a little, visiting the room Spider had been imprisoned in. As they'd guessed, it had a small, barred window facing downtown, recessed in a thick masonry wall.

When she returned to the loading dock, the big doors were open, letting in sunshine from the parking area. The Sasquatches were awake and out of the trailer, huddled against the cinder block wall. Karomeenut squatted nearby, talking soothingly in a language that seemed to consist mostly of trills and clicks. Or maybe he was just making soothing noises. With his shaved head, parachute pants, and tidy tactical gear, he was a huge contrast to their naked, shaggy, filthy appearance.

Ruby stopped a distance away, not wanting to alarm them. "Hi, do you speak any English?" They were from Canada, though. "Or French?"

Karomeenut looked up. "They do not."

"How will you get them back to the compound? Everyone won't fit in your urban assault vehicle, I think?"

"We haf a panel van, but they may not want to go in for a while."

"Understandable. But should those doors be open?"

"They need to thee outdoorth." He touched his earpiece. "Thalali and Reginald will warn if anyone approaches."

"Where are the others?"

The Sasquatch elder waved at the exit. "Your friend left with Derek and that woman." His expression was bitter. "Thpider and Thimon are around."

Simon showed up at that moment in the parking area, spotted her, and came to the big door. He beckoned her over, hoisted himself up, and sat, feet dangling over the edge of the opening. Ruby sat beside him.

"So," he said. "We need a debrief on that operation."

Ruby raised her hand. "I know what you're going to say. But look, I had backup. In fact, I was the backup. Derek went in first."

"You could so easily have gotten yourself killed. And what would I—"

"—tell my parents, I know. But we have a mission. I had to rescue them."

"We don't have a *mission*. We have a *job*. Nobody expects us to succeed or die trying. And you dragged that boy into it, too."

Ruby crossed her arms and scowled at the sunlit pavement. "I didn't drag him in. He volunteered."

"Oh, come on. He follows you around like a puppy. You claim you don't want that kind of influence over him, but you sure don't seem to mind taking advantage of it when you need a, a minion!"

"You should've seen him, though. This wasn't about how he feels about me, he just loves adventure. Marissa was there, too, but she refused to come. She's not such a big fan of action."

"Which shows excellent sense. I'd like you to develop some. There's no point in ordering you to act in a certain way, but maybe you could consider your poor uncle who's going prematurely gray from the constant scares."

Ruby gave him a sideways glance. "I can't say I'm sorry we saved them. You definitely wouldn't have made it in time."

Simon sighed. "Yes, I imagine the Sasquatches will give us a big bonus for that."

"So sad."

"It is sad because it's teaching you the wrong lesson. Remember Russian Roulette? Everybody who continually risks their life has an unbroken winning streak until the first loss. Winning this time means nothing for the future."

"I don't plan to rely on luck. I'm learning to fight."

"And your five weeks of martial arts training was useful in this situation, was it?"

"Actually, yes, I made a very fine fencing move which took down a bad guy, Mister Sarcastic. And Speck was helpful, too." Hearing his name, Ruby's airy pet popped up in front of her face. She waved him away. "Tube, Speck. See, I've trained him to do a bunch of useful things."

Simon glanced at the tube. "He can fly through things, can't he?"

"When he wants to. Or he can bump or bite when he wants."

"That's a pretty powerful weapon. Could he materialize inside someone and start biting?"

"Ick. I suppose, but I don't want to kill anyone. Anyway, I don't know how I'd train him for that. He seems smarter than a regular dog, but I can't just tell him what I want."

"He can live in that state indefinitely? As I recall, he was pretty old and not in the best of health, before."

"Teela said he didn't need to eat—he just likes to. I think he's kind of… suspended. Not sure what'll happen if he ever passes back through the hoop."

"Hm. Anyway. Subject at hand. You're young. The part of your brain that makes judgments is still developing. It's science—look it up. But I know you can figure out when you're about to do something I would disapprove of. Would you at least call me first so I can talk you out of it?"

"Did you even check your phone? How many voicemails and texts did I leave you before I came over here? Listen, when my generation makes a phone call, it's urgent. Answer it!"

"All right. If I possibly can. This time, my phone was turned off in case anyone was tracking it." He twisted to look at the Sasquatches. "I don't know how much longer we'll be here. Those guys would be much happier in Bigfootville if Karomeenut can persuade them to go, but I understand them being shy of trucks at the moment."

"Hm. Hey, I had an idea for the negotiations, from what I found out visiting the Skohlars."

"You think this is a good time to remind me of your sneaking out?"

"Yeah but listen. They trust people more if their names mean something. I think if each of our people explain to them what their names mean, it might make things a little easier. I've been looking them up on baby names websites. By the way, the Internet now thinks I'm pregnant. Do you know what 'Simon' means?"

"I admit I've never bothered to find out."

"It means 'snub-nosed.' Which compared to a Skohlar, you really are. I don't know what Ekki-whatever Abroft means in his native language, though. Where do Wibbles come from, anyway?"

"Space." Simon looked at his phone. "Don't you have a music lesson in an hour?"

"Honest-to-God space aliens? Are you kidding me? That's huge!"

"Old news for me. Music lesson?"

"Yeah, yeah, I'm going. But look, as long as we're talking about the Skohlars, you know I'll have to go down there again. I should visit all the clans, talk with lots of people. They're a lot more complicated than you thought, aren't they?"

Simon huffed, staring at the brick wall across the parking lot. "They're vicious and unpredictable."

"They're only unpredictable because you don't understand them. It's not just for the negotiations, though that's important. They'll come out to The Scene before long, and they'll need a sort of ambassador who knows them, to explain them to everyone else. And then eventually to the world."

"And you think that'll be you?"

"Do you know someone else they're willing to talk with?"

Simon gave her a sideways look. "I'll discuss it with the others on the negotiating team. We do need the intel."

"Excellent!"

"We'll have to get you tutoring in anthropology, I suppose."

Great, more studying. "I don't have a lot of free time for that, but if we dropped the accounting lessons…."

"Go on with you, then." He shooed her away in the direction of the bus stop.

"See you at dinner?"

"I'll pick something up. Try not to…." He waved a hand.

"I won't."

"And think more about what I said about Kirk. If you really don't want to encourage his obsession with you, have less to do with him."

"Fine, whatever."

Her phone said she had just time to get home to get her guitar, then to Mrs. Esterhazy's for her lesson. She walked past the scrapyard and saw Earl inside, talking with a large black woman in a red dress. He looked up at her but showed no sign of recognition.

Totally unfair.

On the bus she stared out the window, not really seeing the world going by outside. What *about* Kirk, then? Did Simon have a point? She really *didn't* want him for a boyfriend. But she sort of didn't want Marissa to have him, either? No, that was just silly. If he was interested in Marissa, fine, but Ruby couldn't force him to be. It wasn't on her.

At home, she dodged around Danno on the stairs—he was fixing a loose banister—grabbed the guitar, and headed down again. She'd gotten lucky with the buses and had a few extra minutes, so she ducked into the study for a brief confab with Micah. She displayed her sketchpad to the ex-rock star's skull on the mantelpiece. "I've drawn you a rooftop shelter. These decorations are gold because why not? I don't need to build it anyway, right?" Something colorful farther down the mantel caught her eye—Retractable Blade's vest and earring. She'd return them next time she was down there.

"Who are you talking to?" Danno stood in the study door, screwdriver in hand.

"This guy."

"That's just a skull. I'm, uh, not sure he can hear you."

"You might be surprised. Anyway, I've gotta go. Simon's getting takeout for dinner."

"There's lots of food here. I could cook something—you know, like, healthier."

Ruby shrugged on her guitar strap. "Call him and ask. He's just waiting around, so he might even answer. Really gotta go. Thanks for fixing the stairs."

She hurried out the front door, pulling to make it click, turned to leave… and found Marissa sitting on the concrete block at the base of the steps, staring at her. Her eyes were red, cheeks puffy.

Well, shit.

Marissa sniffled and wiped her nose on the shoulder of her t-shirt. "Got your text. Thanks for letting me know everyone's okay."

"Um, sure." Ruby chose a step to sit on that would put her at eye level. "Are you okay?"

"Really, Ruby, why don't you want me to have him?"

That was an annoying question. She opened her mouth to repeat what she'd come up with on the bus, but with her friend sitting right in front of her, she just couldn't. It sounded too much like an excuse. "I do want you to have him," she said at last, but she could feel it was untrue even as the words came out.

Marissa's look said she also heard how weak it was. "You certainly didn't seem sympathetic when I told you about the all-robot coffee date."

"I want you to be happy, M, I just don't get dating. You know that."

"You don't have to *understand* what I want to want it for me and be sad if it doesn't work out. And you could help, but you just don't. I've been trying to be the exciting person he wants, you know? With the hair and clothes and so on. You could, I don't know, aim him at me a little."

"You have to be yourself, M, or what's the point? I wouldn't change to please a guy."

"Yeah, I get that about you. But you didn't have to look so pleased when it fell apart."

Had she? Had she looked pleased when Marissa blew up in the coffeeshop? Thinking back, she realized with a sinking feeling that she probably had. She'd felt... satisfaction. And that was an ugly thing to know about herself. She'd been a bad friend. Not only had she not done what she could to help Marissa out, she'd really kind of sabotaged her. Because she'd known—of course she'd known—that Marissa would be totally against the rescue mission. She'd known—of course—that Marissa arguing against an adventure would make her the sort of girlfriend Kirk didn't want. And she hadn't even thought about how to avoid that confrontation. Maybe there hadn't been a better way because the only other thing she could come up with now was getting Kirk's help without Marissa's knowledge, and secrets were no good either. But the point was, she hadn't considered alternatives at the time. It was all just about what she wanted in that moment.

Marissa wiped at her face. "So what is it you want, Ruby? How would me and Kirk being together be bad for you?"

"I don't *know*, M! I'm sorry. I feel like shit!"

"Pretend you did know, what would it be?"

Ruby took a deep breath and buried her face in her hands. Marissa waited.

What would it be like if they were together? She'd seen couples before, in school. It was like nothing else in the world existed for them. Marissa and Kirk would be going off and doing things without her. They'd have secrets from her.

She raised her head. "I would be on the outside. Alone. Again."

Marissa looked her in the eye, still waiting.

"I don't want a boyfriend, M, but I want *friends*."

"You know, Kirk loves all your weirdness and adventures. I can't offer him that. Even if we were a couple, he would totally still be your...."

"Minion?"

"Kinda, yeah. And you and I, BFFs, right? I'd still tell you everything."

"I hope not *everything.*"

Marissa rolled her eyes. "You've gotta make a joke of it."

"Sorry, sorry. Yeah, BFFs, of course. Though I don't feel like I deserve it. I really didn't mean to—"

Marissa waved this away. "Just don't do it again. Not that it matters since you know and I know I'm not what he wants." She stood. "You have a guitar, so I assume you've got music lessons."

A block down, Ruby's bus was pulling away from the curb. "Damn, I'm gonna be late."

"I'll walk you to the bus stop." Marissa held out a hand.

Ruby grabbed the guitar case, and they held hands down the sidewalk, not hurrying since they had at least fifteen minutes until the next one.

"I'll find you someone else," Ruby said.

"Eh, maybe I don't need anyone. He'd just get in the way. I'm going to Mars, you know. He'd want to come along, and there's not room in my luggage."

"Good point. I've always thought men were more trouble than they were worth."

Marissa nodded. "Occasionally useful, but not for every day."

"Exactly. I suppose if you did want one, though, you could do a tweak. I mean, even if you're not 'The One' you have something going on there."

"Nope. Doesn't work if it's about me, remember? I could try and find the right guy for you, though. Or gal or whatever."

Ruby shook her head. "I'm good. Plus it seems like your tweaks never turn out quite the way you wanted."

"There is that."

Ten

The last part of the passage was tight, and Ruby crawled some distance. Finally Retractable Blade's fuzzy butt led her through a rough opening into a larger space lit with bare bulbs, the Old Soldier's Home of the Skohlars. There was one wall of thick pipes and three of cinder block with a metal door blocked and partly covered with Skohlar apartments—a blobby stack of colorfully painted adobe with ramps and round openings.

The floor around the structure was laid out similarly to other communities she'd seen, with little tables, fight pens, climbing structures, piles of equipment, but no merchants. Two of the fight pens were occupied by sparring Skohlars, and many of the tables were in use for tiny board games and crafts. When she entered and straightened up, every eye in the room turned toward her, fifty or so snouts pointed at her.

Retractable Blade went ahead of her, displaying his badge and shouting "Official business! As you were!" He climbed a set of bars and looked around, then dropped and scurried among the tables to lead a particular Skohlar out to where Ruby squatted.

All these Skohlars were old, probably six years or more. Their coats were shaggy or bald in spots, snouts and ears gone white, and some had clouded eyes. The specimen Retractable Blade had selected was among the oldest, the fur on his head quite white, but his eyes were still clear and alert. There was a bump on his shoulder, but he was otherwise healthy looking, still muscular, though a bit slow. He looked up at her and tugged on his vest, pink satin covered in metallic embroidery.

Retractable Blade ushered him a little closer. "Uncle, this is Ruby. She's here to make you an offer. Ruby, this is Sharp Edges."

"Wait, this is your uncle?"

Retractable Blade waved an arm. "These are all my uncles and aunts. They're in my clan."

Ah. Not a literal uncle, then, or maybe he was, who knew? "All right. Sharp Edges, I'm glad to meet you."

He looked at her, narrow eyed. "How are you allowed here?"

"The Cheddar is my friend, sort of, I guess. We get along. I asked him if I could ask you this, and he said okay."

"If the Cheddar commands, I will of course obey."

Retractable Blade held up a paw. "This is your choice. The Cheddar does not command you, only asks you listen."

"Then speak." The old soldier drew himself up and looked Ruby in the eye.

"I understand you don't have long to live." This was one of the refreshing things about Skohlars—you didn't need to sugar-coat things.

Sharp Edges nodded and reached across his chest to point at his hump. "This is growing and will soon end me."

A tumor, then. Cancer. "I think I can help you live longer and also make you an awesome fighter again."

"I would enjoy that. What is my part in the agreement? I would have to serve you?"

With Skohlars, it was always about the agreement. "Not me, but my cousin." Did Skohlars know who their cousins were? The ones who were related on their mother's side should know each other. "My mother's sister's son, Charlie. He's in a place full of enemies and needs a defender."

"If you can do as you claim, I will gladly slay his enemies."

"No, no! No slaying. In fact you have to promise you won't seriously harm anyone. Just scare them. A little biting is okay. The idea is to make them stop bullying him."

"Can your cousin not defend himself? What does this name mean, Charlie?"

"It's really Charles, which means a free man, but he's not free yet. He's just a little boy. Someday he'll be big enough to fight for himself, but the boys who bother him at his school are older and stronger."

Sharp Edges scowled. "That's dishonorable. They need a lesson in manners."

"And you can teach it."

"You can really do this thing? How?"

"I'm not completely sure it'll work, but here." She held out her finger. "Speck, perch."

Speck came out of his tube and dropped to hover above her finger, a barely visible shimmer in the brightly lit chamber. "This was a small dog. Well, bigger than you but small for a dog. He was ill and old, but he's full of energy now, and he can fight. I give him, um, S-N-A-C-K-S sometimes." Better not to say a word that would get Speck excited. "But he doesn't seem to need them. He understands commands like a regular dog would, so I think you'd still be able to understand people talking to you, but he never makes any noise, so I don't think you could talk back."

Sharp Edges moved closer to examine Speck. "I would be able to fight again? And fly?"

"Fly through walls, even. But again, I only know for sure it works on this one dog, and you probably couldn't change back to normal if you didn't like it. But he seems happy."

"I could still die if I didn't like to live in this way?"

Ruby's experiments with poking her own fingers through the hoop had left them "asleep" and tingly for minutes. Doing that to her whole body...? "Trying to return you to normal would probably kill you, so yes, I guess so."

Retractable Blade put a paw on the old warrior's foreleg. "What do you think, Uncle?"

"A new adventure?" He gave Ruby a sly look. "Why not? I'm bored in this place. What do I need to do?"

The End

Are you on the Scene?

the Goodnight Agency

Find out more about Ruby, Simon, and their peculiar clients at https://tylertork.com/gn2

or scan the code with your phone!

Techie guy by day, crime fighter by night. But when crime is slow, as it often is in his quiet hometown of Plymouth, Minnesota, Tyler puts away the mask, cape, and ocelot, and finds a corner to scribble in. The victim of a dark destiny, he whirls through life with a set of shaky assumptions and a mug of rapidly-cooling java. Bewildered, scattered, querulous (some say curmudgeonly), he nonetheless attempts to entertain and inform. Someday, his alien masters will return for him. Until then, buy his books.